I0629910

QUICK SAND ......How do you let go of a past so deep,

That brought you painful secrets that you will always keep

Teary eyes appear from different snippets you try to forget,

You keep telling yourself "I have no regrets".

You try your best to keep those closed doors shut,

But things in your present continue to bring your past up.

The drama you created, the beds you've made,

The people you lied to, the prayers you prayed.

Chasing this money should never have been the plan,

Cause every time I try to go a different direction

I step into QUICK SAND.

BY TANYA "JOURNEY SPEAKS" BAKER.

The Life

Dam… Here I am deep in the hood of Atlanta's East point. Kenny and I are here to pick up a package to take back to New Jersey. The price is right but the situation looks real bad. I guess all cities have their own neighborhood where it's unsafe to go, and this is definitely one of them. As Kenny and I sit here in the car, parked on this dark corner, we are on full alert. Keeping an eye out for any bullshit that might come our way. That's when we noticed a little kid riding a Huffy BMX bike slowly in our direction. At first he rides past us, then make a u-turn and pulls up beside our car. "You the man from up north shawty?" asked the little dude. He had to be no older than 12-13 years old. "Yeah lil man, I'm here to see Gutta, we got some business." I said with a slight smirk on my face. The little guy pulled out a walky-talky, "Yeah, it's them." He said into the walky-talky. "Show them the way up to the third floor." A voice responded. The little guy pointed towards an old looking building across from where Kenny and I were parked. As we both entered the abandoned warehouse there were three guys at the elevator strapped with M-16 rifles, the same ones the military use. "These boys are not joking." Devon said under his breath. One of the guys walked up to Kenny and started patting him down. "Hold up man, we are just here to take care of some business, we don't have time for all this touchy feely   shit." said Devon.

"Whatever shawty. Go on up and there better not be any bullshit or you wont make it back down." The other armed guy said with a toothless grin on his face. Kenny and I walk into the elevator, "Ken, you got your pistol right?" I asked as he reached into his boot. "Yeah dog, you just make sure you take your safety of this time." Kenny whispered. "Kenny, that happened only one time, let it go man." "When we get up here just be cool, we make the exchange and we're gone." I said pulling the Glock 40 tapped between my shoulder blades.

As the elevator stopped at the third floor, I noticed that there was Gutta and some of his body guards sitting at a table at the far end of the room. There was only a single light bulb over them; the   rest of the room was dark. We walked towards them; Kenny whispered "look up". I looked up and I see little faint green lights, it had to be five, maybe six of them. Gutta has some of his body guards in the rafters with night vision goggles. "This slick ass motha…" I said under my breath. "Hey Gutta, can we gets some lights on in this place or what?" I yelled as we walked closer.

"Welcome to the "A" playa. Your hands look pretty dam empty, wait don't tell me the money is in a safe place close by right?" Gutta said. I have never seen Gutta before tonight but as I looked closer, this guy has a mouth full of Platinum teeth. I mean dam, is it that serious, but I had to stay focused.

"Yeah, Gutta you got a nice spot here but why is it so dam dark   in here? You got to pay the light bill baby boy." I said in a jokingly manner. I walked up to the table to shake his hand. "Hey man, let your people know to take it easy, it's all good. We have the money, you have the product?" I said. Kenny and I unzipped our jackets to reveal a vest full of cash, both holding $250,000 each. As we put the vest containing the cash on the table, Gutta's body guards placed two big Gucci suit cases on the table. Kenny walked over to the table and opened one of the suite cases. When Kenny opened the case it was full of Gold metal flour, still in the packaging from the store shelves. "What is this shit Gutta?" I said. "That's your package nigga…..flour!" Gutta said laughing. "Yo, you playing games homie!" Kenny yelled. I had   to calm Kenny down by intervening "Gutta, listen we are here to take care of business. The flour shit …ha ha very funny, but let's get back to business. Straight up, no games." I said in a calm voice. Gutta was winding down on his laughter, "Here is your shit. I wanted to see if you would fall for it." Gutta said. Gutta is one of those wanna be funny guys, but will kill you in a heartbeat. I had to stay calm and keep Kenny calm. One of the body guards placed two duffle bags on the table. Kenny checked out the product to make sure it was the real deal. "Yeah, it's prime time." Kenny said after testing the powder. I then counted to make sure all the bricks were present and accounted for. Gutta sat back sucking his Platinum teeth, looking at Kenny. "Why your   man got to have his chest all swollen for?" Gutta asked with a crazy look on his face. "What, you think this a game?" Kenny said in a mono toned voice. There was a brief silence. Simultaneously, as I reached over to calm Kenny down, Kenny pulled out his gun and started firing. One bullet hit Gutta in the head killing him instantly. After realizing it was on, I pulled out my Glock 40. I fired hitting two of Gutta's body guards. I then grabbed two m-16 rifles from the dead guards hands just as the guards in the rafters started firing down at us. Kenny grabbed the money and the two duffle bags as I fired into the rafters providing cover for our get away. As we dove into the elevator, a few shots hit the duffle bags. I immediately hit the button for the 2nd floor, as some of the guards were running towards the elevator door. I continued to press the button frantically to close the doors. One of the guards got to the doors before they closed and tried to open the partially closed doors. As he tried to pull the doors open Kenny fired a shot into his head. As the doors closed we regrouped and reloaded. We got off the elevator on the second floor cautiously and noticed that a construction refuse tube in a window across the large room. We both figure that the tube lead down street level. We ran across the room towards the refuse tube and jumped in one after the other just as the rest of the guards arrived on the second floor. As Kenny and I slid down the refuse tube, I hit the trunk release to open the   trunk. Kenny exited the tube first running to the car throwing the money and the drugs in the trunk. We both jumped into the car and sped down the street, jumped on the expressway. After about 15- 20 minutes of driving, we pulled into the parking garage next to Underground Atlanta. It is an underground mall, down town Atlanta. We then switched from the car to a black Expedition truck. After wiping down all possible finger prints, we jumped back on the expressway towards I-285 north and got the hell outta there.

After a long 13 hour drive, I noticed that we were getting close to Delaware. I made a call to this white chick who handled things for me. The phone rang three or four times before she answered. "Hello…" she answered. "It's me Devon. I need to dump a car, what do you have there?" I asked. "I have a Camry, how far are you?" she asked. "About ten minutes… have it ready." I said before hanging up. When we arrived at her house, we pulled straight into the opened garage, next to the Camry she had warming up. Kenny took the duffels bags and the money and stuffed them into the Camry's truck. The white chick was standing in the door way of the garage. "Thanks Hun…" I said tossing her $500. I gave her a peck on the cheek and a smack on the ass. Kenny and I jumped into the Camry and headed towards New Jersey, where I had a motel room reserved for the night. We set a time and date to meet back up to split up this cash. After Kenny   left, I laid across the bed starring at the ceiling, trying to fall asleep. I finally fell asleep some time later, only to dream about how I need to change my way of life. I need to go straight or find a new hustle, but I prefer to just go legit. I have an appointment in Atlantic City on the next day; it could be a fresh start. Hell, it's worth a shot. After going through what I just went through in Atlanta, I need to move on from this. Almost getting shot, and taking another person's life….man there has to be a better way, a better life to live. I have got to get out of this life.

Looking for a better way

Its 10 am, the alarm is going off. I really don't want to get up out of this bed, but today is the day I go to Atlantic City to fill out an application. Taking a shot at being a square. That's someone that works a regular job and lives a regular life. I'm applying to be a casino dealer. I had already took the time to go to Dealers School and graduated. I'm not sure if it's all the bright lights or beautiful women that come from all over the country to gamble or what. One thing for sure is that's the kind of playground I want to be in, fast women, faster money. Yes, let me in baby.

I want to make a good first impression, so I chose my chocolate brown Donna Karen, single breasted suit with matching Christian Louboutin crocodile lace-ups. The dress shirt, Egyptian cotton, also by Donna Karen with silk tie. Just a hint of that new, very expensive cologne, Clive Christian No.1 Pure Perfume for men. Trust me it's on point at $2,350 per bottle. As I finished getting dressed, while looking in the mirror I knew I was killing it. I got whistles and compliments on my way to the car from the neighborhood chicks, just to let me know that I was on point. Atlantic City is just a 15 minute drive from my place, so I have a few minutes to grab something to eat on the way. The sun is shinning bright on this 1ˢᵗ day of June. It's just something about summer weather; the ladies are out in their short and tight clothes. It makes the fellas wash and wax their hot cars to attract them very same ladies. Summer has to be the best time of the year. It just cannot be beat; it puts you in that mood.

After I finished eating, I made my way the casino right near the marina. The casino looked like a castle from the outside. I pulled into the valet area of the casino. I see Mercedes Benzes, Porches, Bentleys, and Ferraris. You name it the car was there. Here I am pulling up in my Acura Vigor next to them. Yeah, I know....but it's clean though. As I make my way through   the front door, you can just smell the money this place is making. My mind is racing, but I need to get my mind focused, getting this job is what is important to me right now. The rent is due, I'm at least 3 months behind on my car note…. Yeah I need this job. But if I'm going to go legit, I need legit money. I made my way to the Human Resource Office and knocked on the door. A soft voiced female says. "Please come in and have a seat." When I entered the office, she had her back to me, looking through some files. Then she turned around and looked at me over the top of her glasses. "Dam…" I said inadvertently. Not sure if I said it out loud but, wow! She had the prettiest hazel eyes, the brightest smile I had ever seen

"Hello, I'm Sky Jones…" she said as she extended her hand to me. "I will be handling your interview this morning." I shook her hand. Now, I have seen some beautiful women in my life but…dam. She was about 5'9, 120 lbs. Sharp dresser, very fly, light skinned women. She was just right in all the right areas. "I'm Devon Prince; it's very nice to meet you." I said after clearing my throat. "Well Mr. Prince let's see here…" she says as she looks through my application and file. "No please, call me Devon..." I added. "O.k. …Devon, I see that you have just recently completed dealer's school. " She said skimming through the papers in the file. "I see you have taken

Blackjack, Craps, and Baccarat. Do you feel comfortable taking your audition today?" she asked pushing her glasses up the bridge of her nose. I knew if I said no, I may blow my chance at this position. But I was still a little nervous. "Sure, I was born ready." I blurted out. I can not believe I said that, can't fold now. "Ok follow me this way please." She said. I followed Ms. Jones to the gaming level of the casino. I couldn't help but notice that she was not wearing a wedding ring. "So tell me, is it Mrs. or Ms. Jones?" I had to ask. "In a week or two my divorce will be finalized but, you can just call me Sky. But for now let's see if you can concentrate on passing this audition." She said in a matter of fact tone.

We reached the pit where all the tables are; Sky walked up to the Pit Boss and told him that I was here for an audition. Blackjack was going to be first.

I took a deep breath, shit it's now or never. I cannot make a mistake in front of the Pit Boss or Sky Jones. I took off my jacket as a walked up to the blackjack table. There were just two players; they were playing big money and losing, so they were sort of glad to see me. I tapped the current dealer on his shoulder to let him know it's time for a break.

As soon as I stepped up to the table, all I can hear from them was, "Oh shit here we go! I hope you are better than the last guy!" they both said collectively.

Whenever a new dealer comes in the players are either happy or mad. Usually mad. "I really hope your better than the last one, he took all of our money." One of the players said. The Pit Boss tells the Floor person, who was in charge of keeping an eye on my game, that I was here for an audition. He was instructed to keep a very close eye on me. The Floor person walked over to me, "Hi, I'll be keeping an eye on you, so don't worry if you make a mistake, just go slow." She said as she counted the chips in the tray on my table. "These players are on a losing streak right now, so they may give you a hard time being a new dealer." She added before walking away.

Going for mine

I started dealing the cards, I hear the players saying ..."Give me an ace." "Give me a face card." After the cards were dealt, none of the players had a hand worth playing. So, I heard more moans and groans about the cards. As I go around the table asking each layer if he wants to hit their cards. One player had a 13, the other had a 16. I had a 7 showing. No one wanted to take a hit, as I turned over I had a 6 underneath, then pulled a third card it was an 8. That gave me a total of 21, I won and they both lost. All hell broke loose; the players were yelling and cursing up a   storm. The next

eleven hands had the same outcome.
After about 25 minutes of them losing
even more than before, the original dealer
returned from his break, and the payers
were happy to see him return.

"Don't take any of that personal, you did
a good job." The Floor person said as the
original dealer took over. On my way out
of the Blackjack Pit, I see Sky gesturing
for me to follow her. I followed her into
the Crap Pit and that audition went just as
well. "Well, Mr. Prince, you did an
excellent job on your auditions today."
She said checking off some boxes on the
forms. "I'm going to send you to get
fitted for your uniform. I give you a call
at home with your schedule for the
week." She said   handing me the work

order for my uniform. I felt good about
my audition and the fact that Sky would
be calling me at home. That will be the
time for me to make my move on that
beauty name Sky Jones.

The sun is now starting to go down, but
before I go home, there is some
unfinished business. I am a complicated
man, money and women are my vices.
First stop is Staci's job. See Staci works
at a men's clothing store, where all the
big ballers shop. High level Casino
Executives buy their suits there. So, Staci
plays an important part in how I dress.
Staci is the type of woman who wants to
be liked, wanted to be part of the crowd.
So, I made her   feel that way at least

once a week. She already had low self esteem issues, and a smoking hot body. She sets me up with the high priced designer suits and all I have to do is take her out from time to time and give her the sex she need at that given time. It keeps everything fair and equal in her mind.

"Hey Staci…not working too hard are you sexy?" I said as I walked into the store. "Devon...Hey baby, glad to see you. We just got a new shipment of merchandise." She says as she hugs me …tightly.   "Come to the back, I'll show you. Brian, watch the shop, I'll be back." She said the cashier. Staci showed me the new shipment. It was the most expensive clothes   from the biggest designers. I'm talking about Gucci, Versace, the list goes on. These clothes are not yet available for sale for another 6 months. "How many can I get Staci?" I asked as I sift though the racks and racks of clothes. "As many as you want, but umm…do you have time to take care of a few things before you leave?" she asked as she unbuttons her blouse. When all was said and done 40 minutes later, I left the shop with 5 suits totaling $20,000 and now, I need a shower.

When I get to my apartment door I can hear my house phone ringing, I rush I. "Hello…" I aid. "Hello can I speak with Mr. Prince please." A female voice responded. "Yes, this is he… I said.

This is Sky Jones; I am calling to give you the work schedule for the week. Your schedule is 8pm to 4am. You will start off the week dealing Blackjack in pit #4. Get in a little earlier and I will get you a temp badge." She said as I jotted the information down. "Ok, have it all. But listen, I don't want to come off too strong, too soon. Would you be interested in joining me for a drink after work tomorrow?" I asked. "Sure, maybe just one. I have a long ride home from A.C." she stated. "Good, then I'll see you tomorrow. Have a good night Ms. Jones." I said just before hanging up the phone.

Time to hit the shower then, out for stop #2. I have to go   check out Kenny.

Kenny is my best friend. We both were born and raised in Philly only one block away from each other. Kenny handles my money from the strippers I run in Philly. And when I have a drug run to make, he rides out with me. He's got my back and I got his back. That's what Philly homies do. There are four main girls, all 22 years old, and are go getters when it comes to my money. They all have tight bodies and I have the connection to the big parties where they make serious money. Kenny takes the request calls for strippers. I set the price depending on the type of party and the numbers of hours the girls are needed. It's very smooth how we have it worked out. These girls are very loyal to me.

They have the –us against the world
mentality, and that's very rare these days.
Customers call to say how many girls
they need and how many hours the girls
will be needed. We then have the
customer wire the money to us, the girls
will be at the location 30 minutes before
the party starts. I've been doing this for
the past 4 years now, no problems,
always happy customers.

I pulled up to Kenny's house, and he is
on the porch talking on the cell phone.
"Sup Devon, I got this call for three
dancers at the Double Tree Hotel
downtown. These white guys are having
a bachelor party." Kenny says. "How
many guys …" I asked "Five guys."
Kenny replied. I   gestured 18. "$1,800

for two hours, anything beyond that is $600 per girl, every additional 30 minutes. Do we have a deal?" Kenny asked the caller. The caller paused for a second and agreed to the terms. The girls make $200 per party. They usually do two to three parties per week so the cash adds up quick for them. The girls keep their own tips so, they do pretty well. Kenny and I split the balance. We stand to make as much as $7,200 per month from the guys. Not bad at all. Kenny and I sit back and have a couple drinks; I collect my take from last month. I hand Kenny his take from the Atlanta deal, and I'm back on the road. On my way back to New Jersey as I think, how much longer will I continue this hustle?

With a subconscious grin, to myself I say,
till the wheels fall off!

I'm not home for more than 10 minutes,
the house phone rings. "Devon its Steve,
how did the job interview go?' Steve is
an old high school buddy of mine. Steve
had his own hustle called Real Estate.
You know buy cheap, sell high as
possible. "Hey Steve, the interview went
great. I got the job." I said. "Hey that's
good news. When do you start?" Steve
blurted. "I'll bring some of my agents
down for some drinks." Steve said.
"Well, I start tomorrow night. But Steve,
don't come down embarrassing me or
yourself man, I know how you do." I
said. I'm not   going to show out

Devon, it's me…Steve!" he said in joking manner. "Shit that's what I mean. Steve you are a wild boy." I stated. "Listen Dev., I got to go. I have this blazing hot date with this new mortgage rep. I'll see you tomorrow." Steve says. "Alright doggie, I'm going to sleep." I said before hanging up the phone

Put In Work

Morning came too soon. Its 10 am, the birds are chirping like crazy. The sun is bright, about 80 degrees, feeling real good. I jump out of bed, do my usual 100 push ups, 100 crunches, and a 1 mile run. I like to stay fit. As I head out the door for my run, Mrs. Foster always seems to be outside every morning. She is my neighbor from across the breeze way. "Good morning Devon. Going for that run this morning?" Mrs. Foster asked. "Hi Mrs. Foster, how are you?" I was forced to ask. See, Mrs. Foster is a 55 year old woman,   who constantly flirts with me. She is married to a big meat head, former football player. Mrs. Foster looks good, but I have to keep my distance despite her flirting. "I'm doing fine Devon." She replied as she adjusted her breast in her bra. All I could do was shake my head, put my head phones on and start my run.

I get back from my run. I hit the shower and get dress. Time to go pay some bills. On my way to the Post Office, I noticed that I'm being followed. It's a black suburban with blacked out windows. The same truck has been following me for the past eight blocks now. I go about my business, when I come out f the post Office; the suburban is double parked next to my car. I   walk towards the truck but it peels off out of the parking area.

The truck did not have a license plate and I couldn't see inside the truck. I immediately checked to make sure my car was o.k. As far as I could see, my car was fine. I' don't understand what the hell is going on, why is this truck following me? Maybe it's nothing, just seems very fishy. So, I went on about my day.

The next stop is the Mall. I need some comfortable black shoes for work tonight. On my way to the Mall I found myself checking my rear view mirror for that black suburban, but nothing. I get to the Mall; I walk into this one shoe store. As I am checking out   the selection the store has, I hear a sweet voice… "Can I help you find something?" As I turned around, there stood a beautiful Latin woman. She was about 5'8, long brown hair, and light brown eyes. Olive complexion and a big round….. Well you get the picture. "Umm, yes do you have these in a size 12?" I asked. "I will check for you, Mr….." she softly asked. "My first name is Devon, and your name is?" I asked even though she had a name badge on. "Porsha, I'll check on that shoe for you." She said as she touched my hand and walked away. When I tell you this woman was fine, I mean fine. She looked to be 21 or maybe 25 years old, no ring on her finger. Needless to say I bought several pairs of   shoes, as well as her number. She will be getting a call from me ASAP. Before I knew it, I had spent so much time in that Mall; it was time to start getting ready for work. I get home, take a quick shower and I just happened to look out of the bathroom window, "Dam…" it's that black suburban again. Shit, I'm starting to get a little worried, why is this truck here? I grabbed some sweat pants and a t-shirt and quickly put them on and run outside. By the time a get outside the truck is gone. "What the hell is going on?" I mumbled to myself. I go back inside to get dressed for work; I don't want to be late.

I arrived at work and   checked the schedule

to verify where I'm working. Pit#4, the blackjack pit. I'm on table #4. I head up to the gaming area and tap out the day shift dealer. There are only three players. There were two men and one woman. I look around to see who the game supervisor will be for tonight. Lisa Harper, I see walking in my direction. Lisa is 5'4, blonde hair, 55year old woman and tough as nails. From what I hear she does not take any shit from anyone. She made that clear as I dealt out the first hand of cards. "If any one gives you a hard time about anything, you let me know." She said while counting the chips in the rack on my table. "You got it Sarge, no problem." I said with a grin. Sarge was a nickname I gave her on the spot. After she finished counting the   chips, it was time for

Sarge to take the first break of the evening. Sarge's replacement was a male supervisor. He also comes over to take a quick count. While he was taking inventory he started a conversation. "Some friends of mine are coming here to party at the casino night club tonight and it's going to be crazy!" he said. As if it was second nature I asked, "Do you guys have any female entertainment lined up for tonight?" A little intrigued he says, "No man, do you know of any chicks that are looking to party?" he asked. As I continued dealing the cards to the players, "How many guys are coming down to party?" I asked. "There are going to be about ten guys all together. "He replied. Doing the math in   my head, I said, "So you are going to need at last five or six girls huh?" Getting excited he says, "Yeah, shit that sounds cool." Now being the business man I am, I had to push the envelope. "We if you want each guy to have his own lady to himself, I could make that happen too. The right girls can make the party much more interesting. If you know what I mean." I said taking a slight pause. Dragging this guy into the deep end of the pool, by tapping into his greed. I could see the wheels turning in his head. "Yeah, yeah that's what I'm talking about. We need that!" he said with enthusiasm. "Relax, I got you covered. But first you have to know that these ladies are top notch. I need to know that you guys are   ready for this caliber of women. What kind of cash are you working with. These girls don't come cheep." I said. I forced him to pump his breaks a little, but I just pulled him deeper into the pool. "You and I both know that the right female entertainment will do what ever it takes to make this the party of the year." I said luring him in. Without hesitation he says, "These guys are loaded, so money will not be an issue." Keeping my composure, while looking to close the deal, "So, what time do you want the girls to be here?" I asked. As he pushed back his cuff to look at his Rolex watch, "About 10 pm should be good." He said. I then looked at my watch, "Ok, you got it. I'll make a call when a go on   break. I'll let you know what the cost is going to be. I replied. Relieved that he secured the entertainment for the night he says, "Thank you bro, you're a life saver. Let me know the price." I make it a point to make it seem like I know a guy who has the girls. I don't want anything to come back to me regarding any hook ups. This casino thing is going to be a gold mine, a real money maker for me and my crew. After a few minutes, it was time for my break. I got his cell number and quickly walked to the cafeteria to call Kenny. "Kenny listen, call this cell number for a job for the girls. The job is here in the casino. Get ten of the sexiest girls together, and hire a limo." I said. "Ok Devon, what are   we charging for this party?" Kenny asked. "These guys are supposed to be loaded so tell them the fee is $5,000, and anything beyond dancing is between them and the girls. Once you have proof of the money get the girls here by 10 pm." I added. "Got it Devon, I'm on it." Kenny said before hanging up. When I got back from my break, I could see that his friends were already here and gambling. I could see one guy on his cell phone. After he finished the call he said,"That's a lot of money, these girls better be good." He sent one of the other guys in their party to wire the cash. About an hour later there was a page on the PA system for someone in their group to go to a house phone and dial zero. One of the guys went   to a house phone and came back to the table and said," The girls are I the club waiting for us." They all collected their chips and gave me a fist bump. Shortly Kenny walked up to my gaming table. "Everything is good and is going as planned." Kenny said. "Ok, I just nee you up there making sure nothing gets out of control." I told Kenny. "Everyone get $300 including you, drop off the $1700 at my place tonight on your way back to Philly." I told Kenny. "You got it Devon." Kenny said as he walked away.

Life gets Complicated

After the first night of working as a casino dealer and I make $1,700 within the first five hours, besides the fact that I'm getting paid by the hour. I think I'm going to like it here! I was day reaming about the possibilities here at this casino when, "Hey Devon my man, I told you I would be here!" Dam. Its loud mouth Steve with a group of realtors. When they get to my table, he proceeds to introduce me to all of the female agents. "Listen Devon, this is Cindy, Veronica, Tracie and Sharon." He says loudly. "All single, no kids. What's more beautiful than that?" He   shouts. Steve is the poster child for male chauvinist pigs.

After sitting down at the table, "Devon, where is the drink girl…I mean who do I have to screw around here to get a drink around here?" Steve shouts as he looked around. "Steve, Steve! Bring it down the volume." I said. "Yeah Devon, your right baby…but we are in a casino, there is noise all over this place. Everyone is making noise." Steve says with a slight slur. Needless to say Steve was starting to draw a lot of attention to himself. Sarge was also taking notice, and dam here she comes. "Hello Sir, is there something I can help you with?" Sarge says to Steve. "Yeah Hun, you can get me a drink." Steve blurted. "Ok. Sir, I will have a waitress here pronto, would you like to have your play rated? Do you have a player's card?" Sarge asked Steve. Steve looked at Sarge with disgust. "My play rated? Rate this!" He whispered flipping Sarge his middle finger. Steve is not a happy drunk. "Steve, come on dog relax. You making it bad for me right now, I'm at work." I told Steve. I was hoping he would calm down, so much for wishful thinking. "Naw Devon, I came here to have a good time. But this short fucker is killing my buzz and shit!" Steve said looking in Sarge's face. "Sir could you please not use profanity, there are other players here and you are disturbing them. Sarge said in a calm voice. Steve then   stood up from his seat. "Fuck them, and fuck you. I'm playing my money just like they are!" Steve yelled. Sarge then sat here clip board down saying, "Sir I understand but could you not use profanity here." Sarge pleaded. "Shit, fuck, dam, shit. I will say whatever I want in this bitch!" Steve said moving closer to Sarge. I could see that Sarge was starting to lose a little control. Her face was turning red, as she called over to Pit Boss. Even the Pit Boss could not get Steve to calm down, so the Pit Boss called for security. Steve was still yelling at Sarge, pointing his finger in the face. "You called five-O on me, you called five-O!" Steve yelled to Sarge. Just like a bad dream but in slow motion, Steve raised his   right hand straight

49

over his head and slapped the daylights out of Sarge. Everyone paused and looked in disbelief. When Sarge got up off the floor, she grabbed Steve by the back of his shirt collar and started kicking his ass. She was left hooking him like... Well, like he slapped the crap out of her. Security had to pull Sarge off of Steve, and it was not easy. Security hand cuffed Steve and had ACPD arrest him for assault and disorderly conduct. Sarge composed herself and went to the nurse's station for a possible broken wrist she received hooking off on Steve's midsection and face. After work I went to the county jail in Mays landing New Jersey. I could not leave Steve in jail even though he   brought it on himself. It's about 5:30 in the morning when Steve is released. "Devon thanks man, I'm really sorry I acted a fool tonight." Steve said as he waited for his property at the window. "Listen you got to learn to calm down, it cost me $1500 to get your ass out of jail. I said to him. "I got you, no problem I'll have it for you this afternoon." Steve says as he receives his belongings. Thoroughly disgusted at Steve, "Just slide it under my door if I'm not home and don't forget to do it." I said. "No problem, but can you give me a ride to my car back at the casino?' Steve begged. After taking Steve to his car, I headed home. I pulled up to my apartment and at the corner of my building was that   black suburban. I got out o my car and walked towards the truck, again it sped off, speeding past me. "What the hell is this shit all about?" I mumbled to myself. This is starting to give me a headache. Great, a perfect end to my crazy day.

The next afternoon, I wake up to the sun shining bright and birds chirping. I turn on the television to catch some of the mid-day news on Channel 6. The new anchor says; "This just in, Philadelphia Police Department has been called to 2900 block of North Broad Street. We go live to our correspondent on the scene." As the live shot, the cameraman panned across Philadelphia boxing champ Joe Frazier's former boxing gym. "Yes, we are here near the   former Philly landmark of the legendary boxing gym here on north Broad Street. Just a few yards from that corner, in the shadows of an unused underpass, police were called to this scene. There they say they found a man on fire. He had appeared to be duck taped to a chair and then chained to one of the columns of the underpass and then set ablaze. It is a horrible scene here, we will continue to get further information on what may have happened here and if there are any suspects. Back to you in the studio." Stated the reporter on the scene. I sat up in my bed, still half sleep. I could not believe what I just heard. That has Mr. Stacks written all over it that is his how he deals with people who he wants to get rid of.   Those who know of

Mr. Stacks know he has a very short fuse.
A very scary man.

The telephone starts to ring. "Hello." I
said answering the phone. "Hi, can I
speak to Devon please?" a voice said on
the other end. "Yes, this is he. I said
hesitantly. "Hi, this is Sky Jones calling.
How are you?" I dam near fell out of my
bed. "Hi Sky, How are you?" I
stammered. "I'm ok; I hope I didn't
wake you." No, no it's ok, I was just
getting up anyway." I said still wiping the
sleep from my eyes. "So, how did your
first night dealing go?" she asked. "Well
I think it went well. Why did you hear
something different?" "No, I was just
thinking about you and was concerned.'
She said. "Umm,   Sky let's get together

for lunch or something. We can talk more about it then." I suggested. "Would that be ok with you?" I added. "Sure, that would be fine. Where do you want to meet?" She asked. I thought and one place came to mind. "There is a soul food place called Mama's Place. It's in Sicklerville, we will talk there." "That sounds good, I will see you there." She said. Still reeling from the news report, I had to get my ass in gear. Sky is on the hook and I have to make the most of this opportunity. She will be mine. I feel satisfied that a good first impression was made. But, the first date is key. Sky is a very attractive woman and I intend to make every moment count with her. The restraunt is about   ten minutes from my place, so I have a little time to get my car washed and waxed. As I pulled up to the restraunt, I can see Sky through the window. Dam, she looked good. I mean very tasty, and I was very hungry. As I walked into the restraunt, she stood up, smiled and waved to get my attention. The closer I got to her, her smile widened. "Hi, Devon." She said as she kissed me on both cheeks. "I'm glad we could get together." I said as I sat down. Sky sat across from me, "I took the liberty and ordered drinks." She said. "That's good thanks, Sky." "So, let's talk about you." I said. "Sure, what do you want to know? She asked, sitting up in her seat. "Well, what kind of work have you done before working at the Casino?"

She hesitated, and then said, "I did the modeling thing for a while. Then the video girl spin, nothing panned out for me. Then I met Todd. You know, Mr. Whitmen. I had to stop and think, that name sounds familiar. So I asked, "You mean the Casino President?" "Yeah, a friend introduced me to him at an Industry Party. It had to be about three years ago now." She added as she did the math in her head. "We dated for a little while. He took real good care of me. I mean he paid my rent, my car note and everything. She added. "But Sky, I thought he had a wife and kids." I asked. "Yeah, but he takes care of me and my needs. I'm not   trying to ruin that!"

she blurted. "But Sky, he's an old white man. What could you possibly see in him?" I just had to ask with a disappointing smirk on my face. I couldn't help it. "Listen Devon, he's giving me all kinds of cash. All he wants is the kind of attention that the wifey does not give at home!" She stated in a heated tone. I had to calm her down, "Hold on sexy, I'm not judging you at all. You're a grown woman, get your money boo boo. I just think you deserve better than to be some old man's freak toy." I said. "Look Devon, I'm sorry to yell. But, my life has been hard in the past. Nobody is giving anything for free, shit; I'm using what I got to get what I want out of life." She said with conviction. Then she added, "I started at the Casino as a Front desk Clerk and now I am the Head of Human Resource Department. That's a huge pay increase, from $8 per hour to $40 per hour. He still pays my bills. I'm looking out for me. No one else is going to do that shit. If he wants to do it, I'm going to dam well take it. It's hard enough out here, so what he pays my bills and I break him off a little of this cookie. I'm grown." She says as she finishes her drink. "Devon..." she said in a soft sexy voice. Moving closer to me "....do you think you can handle me?" Without hesitation I moved so close as if I wanted to kiss her. I looked deep into her hazel eyes and said ".....dam right." I could hear her breathing getting heavy, as if

anticipating a passionate kiss. I then
tossed some money to cover the bill,
smiled and walked away.

The ride home I was thinking, this
woman needs someone real in her life. I
planned to be that someone. Her heart is
too cold, hardened by life's problems.
She will be my lady; I just need time and
a plan to get her away from Mr.
Whitmen.

ENTER MR. STACKS

I arrive at my apartment, ready to get some sleep before work tonight. Just as soon as I lie down, the phone rings. I checked the caller I.D., but the number was blocked. I answered the phone anyway. "Hello." The voice on the other end says, "Devon?" "Yeah, who is this?" I asked. Then the voice says, "We have been watching your bitch ass. Mr. Stacks wants the money you owe him, and he wants it tonight! Bring the money down to Chocolate City. And hey Chico, if you know like I know you will be there by midnight." Then there was a dead silence, and then the caller hung up the phone. My past   seems to be catching up to me. But, what money is he talking about, I thought to myself. Needless to say I couldn't sleep at all. I was trying to figure out what money I owed Mr. Stacks. By him being East Coast's biggest kingpin, you don't want to owe someone like that. I started working for Mr.Stacks when I was a freshman in high school. I wanted the hot cars and the sexy girls the drug dealers seemed to attract like flies to shit. I wanted to stay up on the fashion and impress the girls. As far as I was concerned at that time in my life, work was for suckers. I was making two or three thousand per week dealing for Mr. Stacks. Nobody messed with us, not even the cops that patrolled our neighborhood. I was ambitious,

hungry little dude. I was about getting
that doe, by any means. Those were the
good days. Things done changed. I have
seen guys I knew get life in prison or
even killed in shoot outs over turf wars. I
worked for Mr. Stacks for a lot of years,
so I spoke to him a few weeks ago about
getting out the game. Hell, I just wanted
to take the cash I had stashed and just go
legit. I have never been to jail or prison,
and I'm not trying to go either.

On my way to work, I stopped by the
bank where I kept my emergency stash in
a safe deposit box. I took out $50,000
because I'm not sure what I suppose to
owe Mr. Stacks, but the last thing I want
to do is show up empty handed. The last
guy who owed   Mr. Stacks and

didn't pay was found duck taped to a chair in his own front yard and set on fire. Everyone knew or heard of Mr. Stacks, knew that is how he deals with people who owe and the duck tape was his calling card. So, I'm bringing some money with me. This $50,000 is half of what I have been saving for a rainy day, and it's getting real cloudy right now. I grabbed the $50,000 and my Glock 40 from the safe deposit box. I am not taking any chances with meeting at Chocolate City. See, Chocolate City is a night club owned by Mr. Stacks, it's definitely a hood hang out spot. Not to mention it's in the roughest part of city, so being strapped is definitely a must. I put everything in   a nap sack and tossed it into the trunk of my car. I then made a few calls to get some other hood niggas to ride with me in case some extra shit goes down. We pulled up to the nightclub about eight of us. "Ok, everyone wait outside. Give me about 30 minutes. If I'm not back come in blazing." I told the guys before I walked in the club. As I walked into the empty nightclub, I could see Stacks and three of his guys sitting at a table in the middle of the dance floor counting a pile of money. "Devon...what's up baby boy? Come over and have a seat, let's talk." Mr. Stacks said as he poured me a drink of Hennessy Black. "Hey Mr. Stacks, I got a call saying that I owe you some money. I don't understand   what or why I owe you money." I stated as I sat down at the table. Mr. Stacks is a light skinned, heavy set guy. He weighed about 300lbs. He has a scar across his forehead from a rival dealer with a baseball bat. It was a drug deal gone badly. Word is that Stacks beat the guy to death; duck taped his wrist to his ankles and set him on fire. "Devon, I'm hearing things. I'm hearing you want to leave the family." Stacks said as he lights a cigar. "I don't understand why. You have made a lot of dam money with this family." Stacks added. "You had nothing when you came to me, now you have money falling out of your dam pockets. Now….you want to leave?" He said. Feeling to tension, "Mr. Stacks I have made you a   lot of money. I never got caught dirty, never cost you any money. I just want to get out on a clean and clear note. I need to make an exit before I end up in prison or even worst, dead." I said sitting up in the chair. Mr. Stacks leaning back in his chair, "You right, you have been a good earner. That's why I'm offering you a position as a Lieutenant in this family." I had to pause for a moment. "As good as that sounds, I have to move on. I have a legit job and I'm just trying to make a clean break." I said. Now I know there is very little chance of there being a clean break in this business, but it is worth a try. Mr. Stacks stood up from his chair, poured himself another drink, puffed on his cigar.   "Devon, why do you want to hurt me like this? I hate to see your leave the family." Stacks said rubbing his chin. He then continued. "How much money do you have for this…clean break?" He said with a slight grin. "Well, how much would a clean break cost…" I asked. "NO Devon!" "How much do you have?" Mr. Stacks asked yelling. Being caught off guard, I said, "I have $30,000. Its close by, that's all I have Stacks." "Well, it's a start, ill be in touch about the rest of what you owe." Stacks said in a calm voice. "Mr. Stacks, before I leave, how much do I owe you?" I asked. "Devon, remember that Atlanta run you made for me?" Stacks asked with a stern tone. "Um, yeah things got a   little hectic and there were some shots fired. That slimy ass Gutta initiated that bullshit, and he was dealt with accordingly." I replied. "Devon, Gutta was not only one of my top suppliers out of Atlanta, he was my brother in-law. Your stupid, trigger happy, ass killed my brother in-law. But, more important to me, you killed a top supplier. For that you owe. You owe me big time. Now get the fuck out of my club!" Mr. Stacks yelled as he finished his drink.

When I walked out of the club, I thought this would be over. But, it's not, not yet anyway. Here I have $20,000 to make something happen. I still have to replace the $30,000 I promised Mr. Stacks. He left me with the   understanding that no matter what the balance is, I'm going to end up duck taped to a dam chair. That's not a good thing. It's time to shift my hustle into second gear; I have to get this money right. After looking at my watch, I realize it almost time for my shift at the casino to start, got to hurry. I gave each guy that had my back that night $200 each and they went on their way.

The Mark: Mr. Whitmen

The work day went pretty quickly. It was towards the end of my shift when a co-worker asked if I was going to the company party. I wasn't really interested in that sort of thing but, time is money and I want to make some at this party. At that moment I noticed the Casino Executives were making their rounds through the gaming area. Wouldn't you know it; with them was the Casino President Alfonse Whitman, The Mr. Whitman. He favored John Travolta with salt and pepper hair. He had to be at least 6'5 and was clean shaved. Wearing a $5,000 black with grey pin stripped suit. I know because I   have the very same suit. The dude was fly for a white man, I had to admit. I can see the flash that would attract Sky, but she deservers better. Someone that will love her from the heart, and not from the wallet.

As Mr. Whitman walked near my gaming table I aid, "Hello Mr. Whitman." Just to get his attention. "Well hello…..Devon." he said as he looked at my name badge. "You're on of our new casino dealers' right?" he added as he reached across the table to shake my hand. I gave him a firm hand shake. "Nice grip there guy. You must be weightlifter." He asked. "Yeah I work out a little." I responded with a puzzled look on my face. Why would he take noticed of, if I worked out or not? "Listen   Devon, we will see you at the company party right?" he asked. But before I could answer he walked away. I observed Mr. Whitman as he walked away speaking to other dealers, mainly female dealers. I could tell that he had a weakness for pretty women. Time to set a game plan; I have to use this to my advantage. So, yes I will be going to this company party, I wouldn't miss it fir the world.

Finally the shift is over; I can see the other dealers coming in the next shift. As I walked out of the casino area, towards the bar in the main lobby, I noticed woman staring at me. She was Spanish, with an olive complexion. She looked to be about 5'6 and curly long brown hair. So, I walked over   to the bar and introduced myself. "Hello, I couldn't help but noticed you looking at me. My name is Devon. What is your name?" I said looking into her eyes. "Hey Poppi, my name is Rosa." She said extending her hand. "Are you here alone?" I asked. I didn't want to get caught out there talking to this woman and her boy friend gets upset or something. "I sure am baby, you want a date?" she replied. Just then it hit me she is a working girl. So I pumped my brakes. "Listen honey, are you working for a pimp or for yourself?" I asked her. "I work for myself, I am done with a pimp taking all the money while I do all the work." She said while sipping her drink. "Ok baby girl, let's talk about   business later on tonight. Here is my cell number. Call me; I will make you a good offer and better working conditions. Just call and hear me out. Call me around 12 noon if you're interested." I said handing her my number. She took my number and said, "I'll call you, but if you're not buying, move on, you blocking my money right now." All I could do is smile and walk away. I need to get home and get some rest, so I can come up with a plan to get out of this quick sand situation I'm in with Mr. Stacks. Today had come to an end, finally.

It is now the day of the company party. So, I'm on my way to the gym this morning. I have to stop pass to see Staci at the men's clothing store. "Staci, what's going on Hun?" Do you have any clothes in this place?" I asked jokingly. "Devon, you know we get the new stuff first." She replied. "Devon, we don't hook up outside the store anymore." She added. "Staci, Staci baby. You and me, we are cool." I said as I kissed her neck. "We have something that will tarnish or fade Hun. We are a team you and me. Cant no one break that type of bond baby." I said trying my best to sound like Goldie from The Mack. "Now Devon you and I both know that is a bunch of bullshit, but come   on to the back

76

anyway. You lucky I like you." She said grabbing my arm. Needles to say Staci hooked me up with the new selections. The most expensive exotic skin shoes. All she wanted was for me to sex her down in the back storage room. So, I knocked her off and was on my way back to my place. I had to drop off the clothes and shoes and take a shower before heading to the gym.

After I returned to my apartment from my workout, I noticed there was a message on my answering machine. The caller I.D. said it was from Kenny. So, without check the actual voice mail, I called Kenny. "Kenny, what's up playa?" I asked. "Devon, there are some new girls looking to get down with the team."

Kenny replied. "Ok, first how do they look?" I asked. "They look good; I sent some pictures to your email. Check them out and let me know what you think." Kenny said excitedly. "Ok Kenny I'll check the pictures out now. I'm going to need some real go getters, not just pretty faces." I said as I hung up. I opened my e-mail to see these girls. What I saw was some of the most beautiful women. All flavors, from the darkest chocolate to the whitest vanilla. There was this one white girl who favored Megan Fox. Right off the bat I knew she was going to be what I needed to make my mark in this casino. I wanted to use this girl to get close to Mr. Whitman. She just had a look about her. So, I called Kenny right away. "Kenny, this white girl that looks like…" and before I could finish. "…Megan Fox right?" Kenny interrupted. "I knew you would like that one." Kenny added while laughing. "Hell yeah, get her here ASAP. I'm putting her in play tonight. The other girls are great too, but I want this girl and three of our stallions here tonight." I told Kenny.

Kenny arrived at my apartment an hour later with three of our regular homerun hitters and the new girl. "Devon, this is Regina Hartford. She is from north-east Philly." Kenny said. "Hi Devon." she said with the biggest smile. "Hey Hun…" I said as if not interested at all. As all the girls   were seated and settled down, I stood in front of them to make my announcement. "Alright ladies, there is a party tonight at a casino. We have to get all the money we can. Your job is to follow my direction to the letter." I said. "You mess this up for me, you lose a lot of money for yourself." I added. "My regular girls know the exactly what I mean. Kenny take the girls to the mall, they need dresses for tonight." I said. "What about the new girl, Regina?" Kenny asked. "Take her measurements; I need some time with her, to go over a few things." I said as I fixed two drinks. I wanted some time with the new girl; I needed to see where her head is at. Is she up to what needs to be done? Does   she have the

80

necessary skills to work with this group?
Regina and I sat, had drinks and talked,
after everyone had left. She said she was
22 years old; she lives with her older
sister and wants to make money for
school. She wants to be a dentist. She
also mentioned that the last man she had
a relationship with was very abusive. She
had finally left him after 2 years. He
showered her with money, so she didn't
have to work, he didn't want her to work.
That was his way of controlling her. As
she continued telling me the story of her
troubled past, tears fell from her eyes.
The pain was strong, and fresh in her
mind. I put my arms around her in an
attempt to console her. I told her it will
be o.k. "You're in good hands now

baby." I said.   She then leaned in for a kiss; she obviously was caught up in the moment. I pulled back for a second, "Listen you are a beautiful woman who deserves to have a man take care of you and treat you with respect and love. But keep in mind, I am not the rebound kind of guy, I'm not that guy." I said looking into her eyes. "I will do you right, if your down for me 100%. But first of all, this is business." I said to her wiping the tears from her eyes. She then proceeded to caress my face and then kiss me. She agreed to the terms of this relationship, so we proceeded with the interview. One thing led to another and clothing became a barrier to a full and complete understanding to   our conversation. So they were removed expeditiously, and we made our way to my bedroom. An hour and ten minutes later, she passed with interview with flying colors and fireworks. Yes, she will definitely fit in with our little stable.

As Kenny and the girls returned from shopping at the mall, I was sitting in the living room in my silk robe, surfing the internet. "Devon, how did everything go, will she be a good fit to the group?" Kenny asked. At the same time, Regina was getting out of the shower. Dripping wet and naked, she walked from the bathroom to my bedroom. "She will do well Kenny. She will definitely be a good fit. I said still searching to web. I suggested that the   girls get some rest

here at the apartment before we head out.
The company party will be staring in a
few hours. It's going to be a long and
profitable night.

After about a two hour power nap, it was
time to get everyone up and on the same
page. I ordered some Italian pasta
dinners from a place near by that
delivered. As everyone was eating, "Ok.
The regular squad knows what they have
to do. Get the guys on the hook to spend
that money, make them feel they are the
only man in the room for you. Regina,
your mark is a man named Mr. Whitmen.
He is a married man who likes to play,
and spend money on the side. So,
whatever he is into, you're into. I need
dirt on this guy. I   need pictures of you

and him together, lipstick on the collar, all that shit." I said. "Here is some weed and a little blow." I added. "I want credit card information, driver license info. Remember don't physically steal anything. He needs to want to see you again. This is a mission that will pay off for everyone, if we all stay on the same page." I continued to ramble. I then called for a limo to come to pick up Kenny and the girls for the party. I'll take my car and meet them there.

We arrived at the party at 1030 p.m. The party was jumping; they had a D.J. and a live band. They had transformed one of the grand ballrooms into a huge nightclub. There must be a thousand employees here   from all departments.

"Alright, let's get to work ladies. Regina, keep an eye out for the Casino President." I said before dismissing the team. I walked over to the bar to get a drink. As I got closer to the bar, I noticed that Sky was sitting at the bar. She was sitting there with some girl friends laughing and joking. I walked over to them. "Hey Sky, how are you?" Sky looked at me with a smile on her face,"Hi Devon, your looking real nice tonight, come have a drink with us." She said. "Ok, ill have whatever you are drinking." I said as I sat next to Sky. She then gave me a big, long hug. She then sat backing her chair while rubbing my thigh. I could tell that she has had a few drinks, and was really feeling buzzed.   "I'm glad you decided to come to the party Devon. Now I have someone to dance with finally." She stated as she looked around for Mr. Whitmen. I leaned in to whisper in her ear, "Sky are you ready to dance?" I asked. "Let's go, I thought you would never ask." She replied. Sky then led me by the arm to the dance floor. She was wearing a red satin, form fitting, strapless dress. It looked like a night gown, or maybe it was wishful thinking. The music was fast, but we were dancing real close and slow. Following her lead I put my hands around her waist. My hands then slowly slid down towards her soft behind. I noticed that she was not wearing any panties at all. Just as I was getting into it,

Kenny taps me on the shoulder.

"Devon, I need to talk to you for a second." He said. "Excuse me Sky, I'm sorry…" I started to say to her. "….No, it's ok, it was starting to get pretty hot over here anyway. I need a drink anyway." she said fanning herself. "He's here, Whitmen just walked in." Kenny said. "Ok, get Regina, have her sit at the end of the bar. Have the bartender serve her tonic and lime only." I said looking at my watch.

Mr. Whitmen was having a rink with some other casino big wigs. I walked up to the group. "Mr. Whitman, hi remember me?" I asked while extending my hand.   "Yes…ye I do. You are one of our newest dealers on the nightshift." He said shaking my hand. "Um, Devon right?" he added. "Yes, you have a good memory sir." I said. "There is someone I would like you to meet. I said. "She wants to be a cocktail server, and wants to meet someone who may be able to help her." I said pointing in her direction. "I see, so let's meet this young lady." Says Mr. Whitmen as he straightens his tie. As we make our way over to the bar, Mr. Whitmen was spraying Banoca Blast breath freshener. "Mr. Whitmen, I would like you to meet …" "Brandi, my name is Brandi, and it's very nice to meet you." Regina blurted out before I could finish. She caught me completely off   guard, but it was quick thinking on her behalf. I'll just roll with it. "Brandi, it's extremely nice to meet you." Mr. Whitmen said kissing her hand. But I noticed that he did not release her hand after the kiss. So, at that moment I excused myself. Giving her a nod, and let her handle her business. From what I can tell this is going to be a good night. All the girls are booed up with someone to give a private party in the hotels rooms. As each girl left the party there was at least ten to fifteen guys following them. So, now that is set. Where is Sky?

It's about 12:30am, time to make my move on Sky. There she was sitting across the room at a table full of her friends. I walked over to her and touched her shoulder, she turned around and I could tell she was happy I came back. Though she was a little tipsy, she wanted to dance some more. So, I took her by the hand to the dance floor. I had to warm her up again. It may have been 10 minutes; she said she was ready to go. "Where do you want to go?" I asked. "I have a suite here at the casino, just in case I couldn't make the drive home." She said. "Ok, I'll walk you to your room.' I said in her ear. This was going to be a hot and sexy next few hours. My plan is to take her on that pleasure train ride until the sun come up. This is my chance to lock Sky down, and make her mine. The team I have here will handle their business, so I can focus my attention on Sky and pleasing her to the max.

I had to play it cool, take it easy. We laughed and talked about people at the party on the way up to her room. The room was on the 20th floor. When we arrived to the room, she took my hand, looked deep into my eyes, and then opened the door. When we walked into the room, it had a sunken Jacuzzi tub in the middle of the living room. She had housekeeping help her out with this because there were candles all around the Jacuzzi tub. As Boys II Men, Teddy P., and Floetry, plays consecutively in the background; Sky pushed me up against the wall of the room and kissed slow and passionately. The mood of it all was so right. Slow kisses turned wild, as Sky and Devon start tearing off each others clothes. Clothes were being   tossed like a salad.

The two paused long enough to get into the
Jacuzzi tub. The water was still hot as if it
was just run. Bubbles were plentiful.
Devon sat in the tub as Sky mounted him.
Sky started to say something, "Don't..."
Devon interrupted her with his index finger
on her lips. Devon slid his index finger
from her lips down between her breast,
down her stomach, and then to her pleasure
zone. As the two continued to kiss
passionately, Sky let out a quivering breathe,
right then Devon knew was had reached her
organism for the first of many times tonight.
"Dam baby…" Sky says. "That was the
quickest I ever did that, your touch is crazy.
But, let me show you something. "She
added. As she shows me around the room,
she pointed out that   there was an upstairs

loft. She led me by the hand upstairs that were made out of what seemed to be glass that had a bluish glow to them. When we reached the top of the stairs that led to the loft, the entire room was encased in glass; I mean you can see a million stars in the sky. The only thing that was in the room was a huge round bed with silk sheets and a black mink cover. The room filled with the slow jams that played throughout the suite. With all of the amenities, all she seems to want was me, and I wanted her. Devon then picks Sky up, her legs wrapped around his waist. He carries her over to the very inviting looking bed. Sky lays Devon on his back as she begins to give him pleasure as if she knew him all her life. The music, the stars, the woman,   the man. You could cut the passion in the air with a knife. The love making lasted two hours. The candles burned themselves out. The silk sheets were drenched with the sweet sweat of love. The pillows were on the other side of the loft. Sky was fast asleep; the love making had been of epic proportion. Devon covered Sky with the mink cover.

The early morning sunlight with the Atlantic City skyline was coming into view. Devin falls asleep. What seemed like minutes, was actually three hours later, Devon opened his eyes. Blinded by the bright sunlight coming through the naked windows. Still a little sweaty from the love making, Devon looks over at Sky, who was still sleeping. She looked so beautiful and peaceful laying there. Devon brushed some of the sweated out curls from her face. Then slipped out of the bed, as to not wake her. As Devon got dress, He picks up the phone to order room service. "Yes this is room 2020. I would like to order strawberries, wheat toast ands a coffee. Can that be delivered at 10:30 this morning?" Devon asked. The voice on the other end stated that it would not be a problem, 10:30 sharp. Devon hung up the phone and then dialed the valet, while looking for his other shoe. "Good morning Sir, I need a cab ASAP, I will be right down." Devon says right before hanging up the phone. Devon left a note next to Sky: "I had a great time. Call me tonight." Devon then hurries down to the waiting cab in the valet area.

The cab pulls up to Devon's apartment, 30minutes later. When Devon opens the door to his place, he notices Kenny and all the girls were scattered around the apartment. Some sleeping on the couch, some sleeping on the floor. They were all over the place. Devon went to the kitchen and grabbed two pans from the cabinet. Banging them together and yelling, "Wake up, wake up. Rise and shine baby! Its time to break bread! Show…Me… The …Money!!" " Devon, Devon what time is it?" Kenny asked as he rubbed his eyes. "Its break bread time baby!" Devon said opening the blinds to the apartment. "Yo, Devon, we had a good night." Kenny stated. "How much did we get bro?" Devon says rubbing his hands together. Kenny opened the hall closet and pulled out a garbage bag. "We pulled at least $12,500 easy. You ready to count it now?" Kenny said. "Yep, let's do it." Devon replied. After Kenny and Devon finished counting the money, the total came out to be $12,950. Everyone was paid $1000 each for one nights work. And I pocketed $6,950. Devon takes his cut and puts it in the safe under the kitchen sink. "Hey, Regina. How did you make out Hun?" Regina was in the bathroom freshening up. "Hook line and sinker. He has got to be the horniest man I ever met!" Regina says coming out of the bathroom. "I got real close to him, jacked him off a little, but I didn't sleep with him. He wants to hook up tonight to   talk about me working at the casino." She added. Devon says while buttering a piece of toast, "Good job with the name change too Regina. It caught me off guard, but good job thinking quick on your feet." "Starting tomorrow, I want you to record every conversation you have with Mr. Whitmen. I need anything and everything that could be used against him. I mean everything from sex, money, and drugs. I want to be able to trap him on all sides of the board. This is chest not checkers. Kenny will get you the recorder and mic that you will need. Just keep me in the loop." Devon said. As Devon pulls Regina closer to him, and looks into her eyes, "Listen, and stay with me and your going to make a lot of money. I believe in you, hell I believe in   us." Devon added."

" Do you believe in us? It's me and you baby. You're my number one girl. Don't let these other chicks out earn you Hun! You are the sizzle, you are! Get that bread baby, get that bread!" Devon said. "You can trust me Devon; I know not to mess up a good thing." Regina states. "…none of these tricks are going to out earn me baby." She added as she grabs Devon's crotch and kisses him. Devon, shocked and caught a little off guard tells everyone that that's all for today and to keep their cell phones on for the next job. Everyone was packing their things to leave, everyone but Regina. Regina was still sitting on the arm of the couch as the rest of the crew left the apartment. "I just want to show my loyalty and appreciation for   letting me be a part of the team. You know, for giving me the hook up on getting this money. I would like to hook you up, if you know what I mean." Regina says. She then stood up and took off all her clothes. All she had on were red pumps. She then walked over to Devon and kissed him from head to crotch. Regina really showed her appreciation, about an hour and a half worth. The next thing Devon realized is he woke up to his apartment door closing. Regina was gone

Foundation: CYA

The sun was bright; the weather was about 75 degrees. It felt great outside! It was a good day to make some money. Here I am standing on the balcony of my apartment, breathing in fresh air butt ass naked. I don't care if someone sees me. The only thing that bothers me is my obsession with money and power. Nobody's perfect. Today, I have to set aside some time to make some investment. The kind of investments that, f I get locked up I'll have some dam options. So, I went to see a buddy of mine who owns a bail bond company in New Jersey. I haven't been over to see his business yet, but now is a good time.

I make my way over the Ben Franklin Bridge, and drive toward A.C. I take the exit for Pleasantville. The bail bonds office was about five or ten minutes from the exit. I parked the car in the side parking lot and walked into the front door. The door chimes going off. My buddy Tank had his head down looking at some files. "Hello, welcome to Tank's bail bonds how can I…"he says as he is looking up. "Well aint this a bitch! How have you been man?" Tank says as he comes from behind his desk. "Man I have been good, real good. How about you homie?" Devon asked. "Bro, just trying to get this paper. Devon, you're just now getting over here to see my shop? I have been here three years already, and business is booming. Shit, have a seat Devon." Tank said. Pulling out a chair to sit, "Well that's one of the reasons why I am here. I need to retain your services just in case something jumps off." Devon said. Tank starting to be concerned asked, "Whoa, whoa Devon. Is everything cool with you? Are you in some kind of trouble?" "No, no, I'm straight right now. I just feel like I need to cover some bases that's all. I just want to have some kind of safety net." Devon said as he wringed his hands. Tank sat back in his chair as he crossed his legs and said," Ok, ok. You know I got your back like a sweater if you need me bro. Let me know what it is you need, and I got you." Devon with a sigh of relief said, "Cool, cool. I appreciate it homie,   Thanks." "So, I just want to leave some cash with….." But Tank abruptly interrupted. "Devon, no man. I got you. No retainer needed. I know you're good for it. You need me, you call me. Cool?" "Cool. Thanks for looking out, bro." Devon said as they briefly hugged. At the very same time some customers were entering the office. "Devon, it was real good seeing you. Don't be a stranger. Remember call me if you need me." Tank said. As Devon stood in the doorway, "I gothcha! I'll get at you in a little bit, aiight?" Now, that I have a safety net in place, its time to move forward with this plan.

The next night, I'm at work at the casino. I see Mr. Whitmen making his daily rounds, and he is headed in my direction. I had to get his attention, I had to speak first. "Mr. Whitmen, how are you today sir?" He turned and looked at my name badge," I'm doing well, Mr. Prince. How is everything with you today?" he asked as he shook my hand from across the blackjack table. Mr. Whitmen took a deep breathe and said, "The young lady in introduced to me the night of the party..." "Yes, I remember..." I stated. While straightening his tie he said, "Well, I will be interviewing her personally tomorrow. For a position here at the casino, I think she will fit in well." When he said that I knew that all was going as planned.

But I needed to get a little closer to Mr. Whitmen. Just as that thought ran through my mind… "Devon, I'm meeting a few friends and business partners over at the casino night club. You should join us. I have some questions about Brandi before the interview tomorrow." Mr. Whitmen stated. "Well, Sir if you're inviting me, I'm there. What time should I be there?" I said giving a thumbs up. With a slight grin he said, "After work. I think you may meet some interesting people." " Then I wouldn't miss it for the world. I'll be there." I replied. Now, for the life of me I don't understand why I was invited. But, if it gets me in the loop. I'm there! After my shift had ended I headed towards the casino night club. The music was pumping   loud, flashing lights and all. The entire club was reserved for a private party. The people that I recognized were Mr. Whitmen, two of the casino shift supervisors, and a few pit bosses. In the middle of all the action were ten strippers from Atlantic City hottest strip club. I then see Mr. Whitmen from the corner of the club gesturing for me to come over. "Devon! Come on over!" he yelled over the music. When I arrived at the table where they all were sitting, the waitress was waiting to take my drink order. "I have rum and coke, in a glass, shaken, not stirred." I always wanted to say that. That's some cool shit to say, but can someone really tell the difference if it was shaken or stirred? "Devon, I want you to meet…" As Mr. Whitmen was introducing me to   everyone, my mind started racing a hundred miles per second. I was sizing Mr. Whitmen up. What he drinks, the fact that he likes strippers. What else can I learn about this guy to maximize my plan. I stayed and chopped it up with them. I may have had three or four drinks. But I it was time to go, it has been about three hours into the party. As I finished off my drink I said, "Mr. Whitmen, I had a great time. Thanks for the invite. Bu, I have to get some sleep for tomorrow." With a slight drunken slur, "Come on Devon, its early! But, I understand, I see you tomorrow." So, I said good night to everyone or better yet, good morning and left. On my way home the dam sun was trying to come up. I cannot wait to get home. I was tired and it was a long night. When I   got home, all I could

110

do was strip naked and lie across my bed and go straight to sleep.

Beep, beep, beep, beep, beep!! Dam, that alarm clock could really be a pain! But, it's a new day and that means there is more money to be made. I jumped out of bed, walked out to my balcony. Taking in a breath of fresh air and stretching, I hear, "Good afternoon Devon, umm nice day….huh?" said Ms. Tony from the apartment under me. Still half sleep and stretching, "It sure is Ms. Tony." I said. Just then I realized that I was butt naked and on medium swollen. "Oh shit, have a good day Ms. Tony. I'm going in now." I said slightly embarrassed. Ms. Tony looked over the top of her sun glasses and said, "A good day just started for me Devon, take care." She had the biggest smile on her face. I then jumped in the shower, thinking if Ms. Tony could hear me having sex through the floors. I never thought about that before. But nothing I can do about that now.

Business

As I get out of the shower, I hear the house phone ringing. "Hello?" I said answering the phone. There was no response. "Hello, who is this?" I asked. Just then a voice on the phone says, "You better watch your back, motherfucka!" Then the phone went dead. "What the hell was that?" I said to myself. I finished getting dress and started to walk out the door, there was Sky getting ready the knock on the door at the same time. "Hey Devon, I was in the neighborhood and noticed your car was parked outside so I figured...." She started to say. I was happy that she was at my door but still a little pissed. "Sky, wow, you really should have   called. I mean you can't just show up at someone's door without calling first what if I had a female here?" "I'm sorry, but it's just that we had such a good time the night of the party. Maybe we can hook up for dinner or something later. Besides, if you had a female over it would be time for her to leave because I'm here now." Sky said with conviction and confidence. Being entertained and yet intrigued by her boldness, all I could say was, "Well maybe we can do breakfast tomorrow morning. I have a meeting after work tonight. Come by after midnight tonight." As I softly caressed her chin and kissed her lips, Sky said, "Ok midnight it is. I'll be back, so be ready." " So you must be off today huh?" I asked looking at my   watch. "Yup! Just going to do me today. A spa treatment, hair, nails. You know girl stuff. I'll see you later." She says while getting into her car. "Ok see you later." I replied while starting my car. As I pulled up to the exit gate of my apartment, I look in my rear view mirror. I see that same black truck. So, I pull into traffic, jumping in front of eighteen wheeler semi-truck. So the black truck could not follow me so easy. I checked my rear view mirror again and the black truck was not in sight. I continued on my way to work. I jumped onto the A.C. Expressway; I look again in my rear view mirror…. "Dam! Shit! What the hell is going on here?" It was that same black truck. It was weaving in and out of traffic. The two of us are now traveling at a high   rate of speed, speeding past the A.C. rest stop. I passed a New Jersey State Trooper on the side of the road checking for speeders. The State Police car then pulls out in pursuit of me and the black truck, while calling for backup. The black truck then clips a mini van, causing the mini van to collide with the patrol car, all as I sped through the toll booth and exits the expressway. I felt it would be safer to take the residential roads to get into the city to get to work. Every few minute still checking my rear view mirror.

I'm at work now and a few hours have past. The Floor person walks over and starts small talk. "Hey, was up?" he says. Still a little distracted about what happen a few hours earlier. "Nothing much, what's going on with you?" I asked. While taking inventor of the chips in the rack on my table, "Some friends of mine are coming here to party at the club tonight and it's going to be wild. I cannot wait; it's going to be crazy!" he said. Like it was second nature I asked. "Do you guys have girls lined up for tonight?" A little intrigued he says, "No man, hey you know of some chicks that are looking to party?" Realigning the deck of cards on the table I say. "How many guys are coming down to party?" Taking a mental note, "There is going to be about….ten guys all together." Doing the math I stated, "It sounds like you guys are going to need at least five or six girls huh?" Pretty excited he says, "Yeah, shit that sounds cool!" Being the business   man that I am I pushed the envelope. "Well if you want each guy to have a girl to himself, I could make that happen too. The right girls make the party much more interesting, if you know what I mean." As I dragged this guy out into the deep end, his eyes started to widen. "Yeah, yeah that's what I'm talking about man. We need that!" he stated with enthusiasm. "Relax, I got you covered. But first let me know what kind of money you guys are working with. These are top notched girl and they don't come cheep. These girls will do what ever is required to make the party jump." I said reeling him into the deep end some more. With out hesitation he added, "These guys are loaded, so money is not going to be an issue."

"That's good, so   what time do you

want the girls here?" I asked. Looking at his watch, "About 10 pm should be good, I'm off work then." Looking at my watch, "Ok you got it. I'll make a call when I go on my break. I'll let you know what the cost is going to be." I replied. Relieved that he secured the entertainment for the night he says, "Thanks bro, you're a life saver. Let me know the price." I always make it seems like I know a guy who has the girls. I don't want anything to come back on me in regards to this hoop up. This casino is going to be a gold mine, a real money maker. My first call was to Kenny. I had to call him from the payphone in the break room. "Ken, wasup. It's Devon." "Hey, wasup Dev?" "Listen, we need ten girls for tonight. The girls we have don't   have a problem taking it to the max. Mix them up black, white and Spanish chicks. Have them dress for the young professional kind of party. I'm paying them $300 plus what ever tips they make from this party. You will get your normal pay. They have to be in the casino by 9:30 tonight." Kenny writing it all down at the checkout registers. He was already at the mall with the girls. "No problem, I'm on it. I'm just finished buying some clothes for the girls now. They will be there on time." Devon looking at his watch realized his break was almost over. "Thanks man lets get this money." When my break was over, I told the floor person what it will cost for the party. "O.k., I spoke with the guy. It's going to be $1,000 per girl. That's not going to be a   problem is it?"

Devon asked. The floor person, excited about the news says, "Hell no! That's perfect. Plus we will be tipping these girls. The guys are going to love this!" Now me being the businessman I am, I'll push the envelope again. "Keep in mind that if the want these girls to stay overnight it's going to be another $1,000 per girl." I added. Doing the math in his head the floor person said. "Wow! They would stay over night too, that's perfect!" Knowing this guy was for real, I gave him Kenny's cell number. "Yeah, just call this number and he will tell you what to do." As the floor person took the number, "Shit man I'm glad I mentioned this to you. This is going to be a great party!" he said. Yup, this was going to be a great day. Just that   quick I made at least

$5,000, with just one phone call. I'm really going to like it here.

Light Drama

I have to stack this money. Not sure what Mr. Stacks is going to take to let me walk away. It was about 10pm when I started seeing my girls on the casino floor. They were with the guys having the party. So, I spoke with a few cocktail servers and arranged that none of the girls are to have alcohol in their drinks. I also had her pass the information on to the other servers. I don't want them drunk tonight. I gave her $50 to make that happen. As the night progressed, the girls were still partying. Kenny was asleep in the limo in the parking garage. He receives a text on his phone. The text says: "HELP ROOM 2112!!!" Kenny jumps out of the limo and sprints full speed to the elevator in the garage area. Runs to the hotel elevator, pushes the button frantically for floor 21. Kenny gets to room 2112, knocks on the door. A drunken guy answers the door sweaty and out of breath. "Yeah, what the fuck you want?" the drunken guys says as his sips more beer. Kenny stepped forward putting his foot in the doorway. "Sir, there has been a complaint about the noise, is everything ok?" Kenny asked as he looks into the room.

As the drunken guy opens the door wider, Kenny punches the guy in the jaw. Knocking him out. Kenny then steps over the guy seeing one of the girls on the floor. "You ok Hun?" he asked her. "No! This fucker started choking me when he couldn't get it up!" she explained. Kenny checked to make sure the guy was still breathing. Then they left the room headed to the valet area. By the time they got to the valet area the other girls were getting into the limo. Kenny called me and told me what had happened, as I was leaving the casino. After hearing what happened, and relieved that the girls were ok, all I could say was" I will meet you all at my apartment."

As I pulled up to my apartment and walked inside. The girls were showering and talking about the party. Kenny and I were in the kitchen counting the money. Paying everyone for the nights work.

I continued counting money I said to Kenny, "You know Kenny; we had a good night tonight. I really think this casino is going to be a real money maker. I just need to figure how to branch out to the other casinos on the boardwalk." "Yeah, just let me know what you need from me to make it happen." Kenny stated as he paid the girls their cut. After the last girl was paid, I made gathered all the girls in the living room and said. "Ladies, we have had a good night. The parties we are going to get will get bigger and pay more. Just hang in there with me. You guys get some rest and keep your phones on for the next party." With that I had the limo take everyone back to Philly. As I lay in my bed, I realized that I missed my date with   Sky. There were no messages on my phones. I fell asleep for what seemed to be ten minutes. BEEP, BEEP, BEEP, BEEP. My alarm clock is going off. Still pretty sleepy, I said to myself. "Dam! These days are starting to blur together. What day is it? Sky didn't call…Shit!!" As I blindly reach for my cell phone, I hit Sky's number on the speed dial. "Hello, hello? Devon is that you!" she says with a hint of attitude. "Hey Sky, it's me. I didn't get a call from you yesterday." I said. A little more upset Sky responded, "You know Devon, I came passed your place. I did not see you car, so I left. I was very upset…" Just then I heard what seemed to be a woman's voice in the background saying. "Sweetie, I'm going to leave now. Thanks for last night   give me a call soon."

To me it sounded like a woman's voice, so I just had to ask. "Who is that, sounds like a woman?" Sky clearing her throat," Oh that was just a friend. After being stood up last night, I didn't want to be alone. So, she stopped by to well, keep me company." Now I was a little shocked, I didn't realize that you were...." Sky interjected, "What gay? I'm not, but I'm an adult. I like to have fun and that's my business!" I realized that she was getting more upset. So in a calming voice I said, "Calm down Sky, It's not what I ever expected to hear you say. But I like it. If that's what makes you happy then that's what I want for you. That's to be happy. Look, I'll make dinner, come by about 8pm." I could hear Sky taking a deep breathe, then she finally says, "Ok, ill see you at 8pm.

I jump out of bed, went to the balcony to get some fresh air. As usual, butt ass naked. I took at good stretch, and then I noticed that black truck parked across the parking lot. I ran back inside; through on some sweat pants and a t-shirt. Ran to the front door to go down to see who was in this black truck. When I opened my front door, this huge guy sucker punches me. I'm not sure how long I was knocked out, but when I came to, Mr. Stacks and two of his body guards were standing in my living room. Mr. Stacks was flipping through my CD collection. He noticed that I has come to, "Devon, Devon,

Devon. You are a good earner. I'm sorry to hear that you want out. Even more so now that I learned you are working in a casino and all. Come on son!! So many possibilities, so many connections that can be made. I tell you what; I except your apologies and give you a second chance." As I struggled to get off the floor I asked. "Second chance? Mr. Stacks, I want out of the drug game. I'll pay you what I owe, but I want out. That's it!!" Just then one of Mr. Stacks body guards put a sawed off shot gun to my head. Mr. Stacks was now thumbing through a GQ magazine, looked up at me and said. "Devon, I want access to that dam casino and you're going to be my man on the inside. If not, then I will have to go see your pretty little   girlfriend. Sky

Jones is her name right? Yeah… Sky Jones. If you don't do what I say, Ms. Jones will be found duck taped to a street light and set on fire. It's your choice. Yeah, I have been keeping a close eye on your ass. It's your choice. You call me tomorrow with your answer." Then he simply put the magazine on the table and walked out of the apartment. Now here I am with a serious problem. I have to find a way out of this mess. A plan to get my money, and get Mr. Stacks off my back for good. I don't want Sky mixed up in this at all.

Devon looked at his watch noticing that it was getting late. Sky would be here in a few hours. "There is nothing here to cook." Devon said under his breath. So, he calls up the Italian restraunt around the corner and had them deliver a meal for two. As he sets the table as if he cooked it all himself, there was a knock at the door. This time he looked through the peep hole. It was Sky. Sky enters as Devon greats her with a peck on the cheek. "Wow, it smells great in here. I didn't realize you were a good cook. But, how does it taste?" She says with a hint of sarcasm. "Shit girl you don't know? You better recognize. Come on in the dinning room and have a seat." Devon countered as he popped his collar. Sky sneaks a pinch of a side dish on the   kitchen counter.

132

"Umm, that's good. You must be a really good cook." She said as she watched Devon pour two glasses of 1787 Chateau Lafite. It is a very expensive bottle of wine going for $160,000, given to him by a wine collector a few years ago. But it seemed to be fitting for this dinner. "There is a lot you don't know about the kid..." Devon replied. Just then Sky walked over a gives me the biggest kiss. At that very moment I had to have her. On the kitchen counter, the living room floor, we were all over the apartment. We broke a lamp, dented the frig. I don't remember how we punched a hole in the drywall but, it is, what it is. The sex was animalistic in nature and lasted 56 minutes.

Moves to be Made

By the time it was all over, we both were
hungry. Time to eat. Here we both are
lying on the living room floor, naked eating
dinner with our hands. "Devon, how do you
feel about me?" Sky asked as she put a piece
of food into her mouth. Devon taking a
drink of his wine, "What do you mean
Hun?" "I mean are we together or, I mean
what are we really doing here?" Devon sat
up. "Sky, I have feelings for you but, what
is going on with you and Mr. Whitmen?" He
asked as he brushed a piece of hair covering
her left eye. "Look, he's just a source of
security that I happen to sleep with from
time to time. It's about survival for me
that's all." She   stated

as she moved closer to Devon. "Yeah, I can understand that Sky. Listen, I want you, but you got to let that guy go." Taking a drink Sky paused and with a slight look of embarrassment. "Devon, I want you in my life. I have expensive taste and he takes care of those needs." " But does he make you happy, I mean truly happy?" Devon blurted his interjection. "Beyond the material things, what does he give of quality, love? Does he love you?" Sky looked at Devon thinking to herself that maybe he was right. Were material things more important to her than love? When did a price tag get put before love and passion?

Waking up early the next morning, Devon dialed Mr. Stacks. Ring, Ring, Ring. Finally Mr. Stacks answered the phone. "Yeah, yeah…who the hell is this? He answered in as if just waking up. "Mr. Stacks, its Devon…." Still half sleep Mr. Stacks grumbled, "This better be some good shit, you waking me up this dam early!" "It is Mr. Stacks. I set up a meeting for you to meet one of the top guys at the casino. Be there about 1:30 pm for the meeting. I'll meet you at the bar in the main lobby" Devon stated as he cleared his throat. Mr. Stacks just chuckled; he just hung up the phone. "Hello…Hello?" Devon said. "This bitch just …hung up the phone…in my ear!" he added under his breath. I then called Mr. Whitmen but was   connected to his voicemail. So, I left a message. "Hello, Mr. Whitmen this is Devon. There is a high roller that I want you to meet. He is interested in playing in your casino and meeting you as well. Please give me a call when you receive this message. Thanks." About 20 minutes later, Mr. Whitmen called back. "Devon, I just received your message. I'll have the Portevino, the Italian restraunt host the meeting. It overlooks the marina, it has a great view. You know Devon you have been working very hard lately. Don't think it has gone unnoticed. You are working your way to a promotion son. If this meeting works out, things could start looking good for you." With fake sincerity, "Mr. Whitmen, I want to get in good with the company. Plus,   I got your back."

Now that everything is set in motion. I need to make sure I get rid of both Stacks and Whitmen's ass for good. All without Sky knowing. Before hanging up Mr. Whitmen added. "Oh Devon, before I forget there is a party tonight in the Penthouse Suite. Nothing big, just a few big wigs getting together for dinner and drinks. I want you to meet some people. The kind of people that could help with your career." I thought carefully, "Yeah, umm. I can't wait to meet them. I'm looking forward to it." Something just did sound right about what he said. Just going to make it work for me. The rest of the day I was just trying to figure out my next move. Before I knew it, it was time to get ready for the party. On the way into Atlantic City, I stopped to get some gas. When I pulled into the station, there was Sky and several of her friends.

"Hey, Sky where are you guys on your way to?" I asked. Sky got out of the car and hugged me. "We are on our way to Mr. Whitmen's Penthouse Party. Are you going?" she asked. "Yeah, I'll be there in a few. I have a couple stops to make first." I said as I pumped my gas. "Ok, I'll see you there. But don't be too long." Sky stated as she jumped back into the car with her friends. "No, no Hun I won't. Just save me a drink." She blew me a kiss as she pulled off.

After I got my gas and a Mountain Dew. I drove to Harrah's Casino to do some gambling and some mental planning. I pulled into the valet area, tossed the valet the keys. I wandered into the casino, I had to relax and not over think this caper. I think ill shoot some dice and order a rum and coke with little ice. Yeah, that sounds real good right about now. As I arrived at the craps table I threw $800 on the table. "Give me $800 in twenty-five dollar chips please." I said as I signaled for the waitress to come over for my drink order. "$800 cash, $800 in cheques out. To new shooter!" The dealer yelled. I just happed to be the next shooter to roll the dice. "Coffee, Tea, Soda….Coffee, Tea, Soda!" The waitress called   out as she approached the craps table.

"What can I get you Hun?" the waitress asked. "Hey, yes I'll have a rum and coke, with a little ice please." I said as I picked up two dice off the table. I then threw the dice against the side wall of the table to get the maximum spin of the roll. "Seven winner, seven winner!" the dealer yelled. I just realized I just won three hundred dollars just that quick. "Double all my bets across the board." I stated to the dealer. I then rolled the dice again, "Winner seven, seven winner!" the dealer yelled again. That was another $1,800 that I won and I hadn't received my first drink yet. Another roll netted me an additional $900, all in the matter of 10 minutes. It was my lucky night. The waitress   returned with my drink. "Here you are Hun." She said handing me the drink. "Thanks, Hun. This is for you." I said handing her a tip. For the next 20 minutes I was winning so much money, I had to leave. It was like a dream. I ended walking away from the table with close to $9,000. So, needless to say it was time to get the hell out of there. Most gamblers would stay and keep playing. The longer you play the odds are in the casino's favor. Don't try to break the casino. The casino with never, ever run out of money. But you will.

"Hey, cash me out please. I'm done." I said to the dealer. I took my chips to the cashier window. She counted out $9,000 in one hundred dollar bills. I pocketed the cash and headed to the party.

The party was packed, and in full swing. As I walked in I see Mr. Whitmen was waving me to come over. "Devon! Come over here. There are some people I want you to meet." He said. As I made my way over to him, I walked through a big cloud of weed smoke. About half way there I ran into Sky who then gave me a hug and kiss. I noticed that Mr. Whitmen was looking at us and he didn't look happy. "Devon, how about a drink, I'm buying?" Mr.Whitmen asked. "Sure, rum and coke is fine." I stated.

Hook: Mr. Whitmen

Smelling like weed he put his arm around me and said," Listen Devon, you are a smart guy. And I like you. But stay away from Sky… She's mine. Ok?" he said as we walked over to the bar.

"So, what will you have Devon?" Thinking about what Mr. Whitmen just said caught me off guard. "Yeah, Yeah, I'll have a rum and coke with a little ice." I said as we stepped up to the bar. Mr. Whitmen was gesturing across the bar. "There are the Senator and the Mayor." he said signaling them to come over. As they both made there way over I had to put my game face on. These two gentlemen were the ones who ran Atlantic City.   "Senator and Mr.

Mayor, I want you to meet Devon. He's a new dealer here at the casino. He's a really bright young man, with high ambitions." Mr. Whitmen said as he puts his hand on my shoulder. "I see, I see. Will he be a part of the team?" asked the Mayor. "The question is, will he be a team player?" asked the Senator while taking a drink. "I assure you guys that he is. He has a meeting with a high roller for tomorrow afternoon." Mr. Whitmen interjected. The Senator smiled and shook my hand. "Good job son, you could be a very valuable part of this team if you keep your eyes open and your mouth shut. You will go far."

As the party carried on Mr. Whitmen and the Senator slipped away from the party.

One after the other. I followed and watched them go into one of the hotel rooms down the hall. I grabbed my cell phone and sent Sky a text: *I want to see you after the party, come to my place.* - Devon.

Sky sent back a response: *O.k. I'll be there about 3am just be ready for me.* –Sky.

On my way down the hall to see what was going on in the room. I could hear them laughing and talking. I pushed the door open just a little, I could see them lying across the bed snorting blow and smoking weed. Something just didn't seem right. They started holding hands with their fingers interlaced, now holding hands is a little suspect but no two men should ever have their dam fingers interlaced….. Oh shit! Just then the   two most powerful men in Atlantic City kissed each other in the mouth. I thought I was going to throw-up and then pass out. As I tried to catch my balance, the door creaked.

Mr. Whitmen jumper up off the bed and yelled, "Who is there!" As he comes to the door, and snatches it open. He looks out into the hallway. He just missed me dip around the corner frantically pressing the call button for the elevator to open. I can hear Mr. Whitmen coming down the hall towards the elevator. Just as he turns the corner to the elevator, I disappear into the elevator pressing the button for the door to close. "Stop, hold that elevator!" he yelled running towards the elevator. The doors close just as he gets to the elevator. I was up against the wall of   the elevator talking to myself and sweating like a pig. "Whoa! That shit was close! That's it.....he's bi-sexual." As if a moment of clarity struck me. "I could use this, Mr. Whitmen and the Senator are gay lovers. They are both putting up this front as if they are straight!"

I went straight to the valet area, got into my car. On the way home I couldn't help but to think that the plan took a slightly different turn. I have to find a way to exploit it.

Knock, knock, knock. It's about 3:30 in the morning when Sky knocked at my door. "It's about time you showed up." I said jokingly. I could tell that she was a little intoxicated. "Well, I hope your ready for me....and my friend." She said with a slight grin on her face. I thought to myself, no she did not bring another woman with her. It's about to be on! "Oh I'm ready; I just didn't count on there being a spectator!" I said opening the front door wider. Just like that, they both led me to the bedroom. Clothes were being tossed all over the room. Let's just say it was a sweet mess in the bedroom. These women left their inhibitions at the door. I got the better of them both thanks to my multi-vitamins and crazy stamina. There were a lot of moaning and groaning through out the night. After being spent of all I had, I fell asleep. You know how that is.

I awoke the next afternoon about 12:30 pm to the smell of pancakes, turkey beacon and scrambled cheese eggs. I hopped up out of

149

bed and walked into the kitchen, not realizing that I was still naked. Sky and her friend were making breakfast in nothing more than thongs. I was in virtual heaven. Sky handed me a tall glass of orange juice. "Hey, Devon. How did you sleep?" she asked giving me a peck on the cheek. "Good, I slept like a baby." I responded. We all sat down to eat breakfast, laughing and trying to remember last night. After eating, I walked out onto the balcony. Sky followed after me. "Did you have fun last night Devon?" "Yes, I did. I have to admit it caught me off guard you showing up with your girlfriend like that." "Yeah, I figured you would be surprised by that, but she and I will have to be going soon. I see you have your energy back   after that breakfast.

It would be a shame to let this right her go to waste." Sky says while stroking my manhood. Just then Sky's friend walked out on the balcony and they both pulled me back into the bedroom. "What a way to start the day!" I said as they closed the bedroom door behind me.

Just as the ladies finished getting dress after that second round TKO and left the apartment, there was a knock at the door. I put on my bath robe to answer it. As I opened the door, one of Mr. Stack's bodyguards pushes his way into the apartment. Mr. Stacks walks in calmly behind him. "Get dress Devon and call your contact at that casino. Make sure we are still on for this meeting today. This better not be any bullshit either." Mr. Stacks said as he looked around the apartment. So, I got dressed and called Mr. Whitmen. The phone rang three times before he answered. "Mr. Whitmen, this is Devon…." "Hey Devon, How are you?" "I'm good, that was one hellava party." I said nervously. "Yeah well thanks for coming…So what can I do for you Devon?"

"Well the high roller I mentioned to you wants to make sure the meeting is still on." "Sure it is, I made sure everything was set." He said. "Good I'll let him know, and we will see you there Mr. Whitmen." I hung up the phone and walked back into the living room. Mr. Stacks was thumbing through one of my GQ magazines sitting on the couch and his bodyguard was in my dam refrigerator drinking orange juice out of the container. "There is such a thing as a glass my man!" I said to the bodyguard. He looked at me as he finished off the carton of orange juice, crushed the carton like a beer can and just dropped it on the kitchen floor. I was pissed. I have to hurry and get these guys out of my apartment. "Ok, Mr. Stacks we are all set for the meeting." "Good, Good, young blood. I'll see you there and don't be late." Stacks said as he smelled one of the cologne samples in the magazine. They were finally gone. Thinking quickly on how I can get this meeting recorded some how. I called Kenny over to set a plan in motion.

The Set Up

Kenny shows up at my apartment about an hour later. "O.k., Devon what do we need to make this plan flawless?' Kenny asked ready to take notes. "Well, let's take what we know so far. Mr. Whitmen likes guys and he likes drugs. Let's have the meeting place set with hidden cameras and microphones…." I said while pacing back and forth. "Now, there is this girl I am checking out. Her brother is a male escort. We can use him to set up some compromising picture and footage with Mr. Whitmen." Kenny interjected. "Yeah, yeah, that's wasup. I need to make a quick call." I said reaching for my cell phone. "Hello, yo this that dude from Jersey. I need to pick up some of that china white." I stated on the phone. The voice on the other end asked," Yo, how much you need?" "A kilo should be good." I said. "Alright, meet me at the Gallery Mall downtown Philly. Upstairs at the shoe spot where they sell the gators shoes. Two hours… (Click)." The voice on the other end said just before hanging up. "O.k. that's done. Now, Mr. Stacks always has his body guard carry his money and drugs in a black steel brief case. I have to get one just like it. Since I know how he bags his drugs we will swap the cases with one that has crushed plaster." I said thinking out loud. "But what happens when someone test the drugs?" Kenny asked. "Mr. Stacks always has one bag extra on the top for testing and   he always adds an extra bag in for making the deal. That bag will be the real bag, the rest will be straight plaster mixed with baking soda. It's a tow fold plan. One: Stacks is made to seem he is selling bullshit and his name will be dirt on the streets…" I told Kenny. "But he can still go down for selling weight….." Kenny added. "Yup, and we get it all on film. And as for the cash that Mr. Whitmen is going to give in exchange…. Hey its finder keeper's losers go to jail. It's all part of collateral damage." I said with a smile.

Kenny was thinking hard about one thing. "How do we use this male escort to set up Mr. Whitmen?" "Well, since he likes guys, we will have them cross paths before the meeting. You know, catch Mr. Whitmen's eye at the bar or something. Have the guy spike his drink and get him back to the room. While he is passed out, stage the room as if something went down…" I said. "Yeah, make it seem like they got busy. Sprinkle some coke on the bed, some empty condom wrappers o the floor. Take mad flicks." Kenny added. "While Mr. Whitmen is knocked out we search the room for the cash. Yeah….Yeah, that's wasup. Let's get this plan into action." I stated looking at the clock. "I'm already on it Devon. What time is this all going down?" He asked. Thinking about the time frame. "Let's have everything set up by 8pm. I'll call Stacks and Whitmen to make sure these guys are there on time.

While I'm getting dressed, I call Mr. Stacks. "Hello, Mr. Stacks. The meeting is all set for tonight with the guy at the casino. He's looking to pick up eight pieces from you. You got it?" I asked. "You sure he wants eight of the grown and sexy ones, cause we need to be sure." Stacks asked. "I'm sure; you might want to bring that extra one like you usually do." I added.

Stacks was getting pissed, he didn't take kindly to anyone telling him what to do. "Look here you little punk; don't tell me how to do my thing. I always show love like that, so I don't need you telling me shit….o.k.?" He shouted. "You got it Mr. Stacks, my bad…." "Dam right your bad, I didn't get to be a dam kingpin listening to little fuckers like you. I live this shit, this aint no dam rap song! What time is the meeting?" Stacks added. "The meeting is at midnight. I'll meet you at the bar in the lobby. He set up a place handle business and talk." I told Stacks as I looked at the clock. "O.k., ill be there. Tell him to have the money ready. I don't have a lot of time." Stacks added. "It will be ready…don't worry …I got you." I said with a smirk on my face.

After hanging up with Stacks, I called Mr. Whitmen. "Mr. Whitmen…?" He was busy signing contracts in his office. "Hey Devon, how's everything going?" "Everything is going good, the meeting is all set for midnight tonight Mr. Whitmen."

"That's good news Devon." "I also took the liberty of reserving the penthouse suite for the meeting also Mr. Whitmen." Mr. Whitmen was distracted busy signing contracts. "Good job Devon, I can see you are going to go far in this business. But right now I'm pretty swamped. I'll see you both at the bar at midnight Devon." "No problem sir, see you then. But I was asked to mention to you Mr. Whitmen to have the money ready." Mr. Whitmen let out a hearty laugh. "Devon, tell him not to worry. He can bring Columbia's entire product, I'll have the cash he needs. If the product is good there will be a lot of business being done and done long term. Look Devon, I have to go, see you tonight."

All is set; Kenny is on his way back to the apartment with the switch case. It is full of dry wall plaster and baking soda and also a kilo of that china white. He met with the guy at the Gallery Mall. Everything is falling right into place. Then the call was placed to make sure the room was set up with a camera and microphones.

A few hours later there was a knock at the door. It was Kenny; he was back from the meeting at the mall. "Devon, we are all set on this end. How are we going to make the switch?" Kenny asked. After Devon checked the case, "Ken, the switch will take place at the bar at midnight. Just leave that up to me. How about the guy you mentioned earlier?" Devon asked. "I just have to tell him what time to be there, he's ready." Kenny stated as he checked he time on his watch. Devon sits down on the couch, "Good have him there at eleven. We need him to make contact with Mr. Whitmen early. Then have him set something up for right after the meeting with Mr. Stacks." On his way out the front door, "Got it, I'll make sure that happens." Kenny said. After Kenny left the apartment, Devon needed to make one more call. Just to make sure all the bases are covered. "Hey…it's all set. The meeting is at midnight. Both of them will be in the penthouse suite with the product." Devon says. A female's voice on the other end, "ok, no problem. Thanks for the info." As Devon   hangs up the phone, pours himself a shot of Hennessey Cognac, "Now, all is set. Just wait for it all to unfold, and watch the chips fall." He says under his breath.

It's now 11pm, the male escort is in place at the bar having a drink. Mr. Whitmen is heading towards the very same bar with two of his assistants. As Mr. Whitmen is briefing his assistants he notices the gentleman making direct eye contact with him at the bar. As the escort notices that Mr. Whitmen has made eye contact, he gives a brief but deliberate smile. "Ok guys, that's all for tonight. Make sure everything is ok with the gaming area. I have a meeting a little later, check back in with me at 3am."

Blindness of Greed

Mr. Whitmen states while maintaining eye contact with the gentleman at the bar. After his assistants went about their duties, Mr. Whitmen walked over to the bar and ordered a drink. The male escort, looking directly at Mr. Whitmen asked, "You come here often?" Looking straight ahead and taking a sip of his drink, "I run this place, and you, are you enjoying yourself here?" Mr. Whitmen asked. Gesturing the bartender for another round, the escort replied. "So far, So good." "Please, bartender, put these drinks on my tab." Mr. Whitmen asked. The escort lifting his glass "Thanks." "Listen my name is Trevor, I'm heading to have dinner, care to join   me?" The escort asked. Looking into the escorts eyes, Mr. Whitmen finished off his drink and said," I would like to but, I have a meeting at midnight. But, where can I find you afterwards?" The male escort smirked and started writing on a bar napkin. "Here is my cell number. Call me as soon as you're done with your meeting. I'll be around." Mr. Whitmen reached for the napkin at the same time the escort held on to the napkin and said, "Call….me." After the escort released the napkin Mr. Whitman laughed, "As soon as I'm done with my meeting, I'll call."

The time now, is 11:45pm. Shortly after Mr. Whitmen walks away from the bar. Mr. Stacks is coming up the escalator. Mr. Stacks walks over and sits at a table near the bar. Sets down the case next to his chair. Devon, who has had a bird's eye view of everything going down, sees Mr. Stacks and makes his way down to greet him. "Hey Mr. Stacks…." Devon says while reaching for a hand shake. Mr. Stacks totally ignoring Devon's extended hand, guesters for the waitress. "Devon, what's up man?" "Just making sure everything goes smooth with this meeting." Devon says as he sits at the table with Mr. Stacks. The waitress makes her way to Mr. Stacks. "Yes sir, what can I get you?" she asked. "Yes, let me have a double shot of Grey Goose. But by the way, what is your name young sexy?" Mr. Stacks asked as he puts his hand on her hip. As He was hitting on the waitress, I had someone in place to   make the switch on the case next to Mr. Stacks. After the switch was made and Mr. Stacks was done flirting with the waitress, Devon took out some cash from his pocket, "Mr. Stacks, I have to go. The drinks are on me; let me know how the meeting turned out." Devon said as he drops fifty dollars on the table. As Devon leaves, and returns to his perch where he can see everything, Mr. Whitmen walks towards Mr. Stacks. Its midnight, right on time. "Hello, Mr. Stacks right?" Mr. Whitmen asks. Mr. Stacks stands up to shake hands with him. "Yes, and you are Mr. Whitmen?" Mr. Stacks says. "Yes, yes. Let's go up to the Penthouse where we can talk business." Mr. Whitmen suggests as he points towards the elevator. From a safe distance there was someone taking   pictures of the two

167

men shaking hands. Photos were taken of the two heading to the elevator, with Mr. Stacks carrying the brief case. The elevator, with a special access card arrived at the Penthouse floor. Mr. Whitmen while opening the door says," Devon says that you have the best coke on the east coast."

"Well, I feel that it is the best out there…" Mr. Stacks states as he sets the briefcase on the coffee table.   The two gentlemen sat across from one another. "That's good to hear. Let's have a sample of the merchandise." Mr. Whitmen says rubbing his hands on his knees. Mr. Stacks as usual, takes a bag off the top to sample from and hands it to Mr. Whitmen.   Mr. Whitmen takes out a small knife, slices into the bag, and takes out a little   powder from the

bag. He sniffs some of the powder in both
nostrils and rubs a little on his upper gum
line. He then sits back, sniffs "That's some
really good stuff, do you care for a drink?"
He asks Mr. Stacks. Mr. Stacks grabbing a
cigar for the cigar box on the table, "Well,
ill have a quick drink. If it's all the same to
you, I really need to get going. So, if we can
finish our business transaction…." Mr.
Stacks says as he lights up the cigar. "No,
no that's cool, I understand. But first, a
toast to a long and profitable business
relationship. Cheers!" As the two men finish
their drinks, Mr. Whitmen goes behind the
bar to retrieve the brief case full of money.
After a quick count of the money, Mr.
Stacks stands up to shake Mr. Whitmen's
hand. "It's good   doing business with

you. Contact me when you need more."
Mr. Stacks says with a smile. "Thanks for
coming personally. I feel good about this. I
will contact you to re-up. Are you ok
finding your way back down to the casino?"
Mr. Whitmen asked. Walking towards the
door Mr. Stacks turns to say, "Sure, I'm
ok…" "Ok good, I need a quick restroom
break. I have to meet someone in a few
minutes." Says Mr. Whitmen as he dances
towards the restroom. Mr. Stacks then
leaves the Penthouse and walks towards the
elevator, feeling good about the transaction.
He presses the button to call for the elevator,
as the doors open; there stand two
uniformed police officers and a female
detective. As if time had frozen for a
second, "Hold it   right there, put down

the case and put your hands up!" yelled the female detective. The officers had guns drawn there was now where Stacks could run. "What the hell is going on here?" Stacks yelled back. The detective takes the case from Stacks as the officers' place handcuffs on Mr. Stacks "We have been watching you Stacks. We have you for distribution of narcotics." The detective says to Mr. Stacks. Stacks could not believe it. After thinking for a second, he figured that Mr. Whitmen must have set him up. "That mother fucker I'm going to kill him!" Stacks yelled.

The officer makes their way to the valet area where the patrol cars were parked. Devon pulls the detective to   the side before she

walks out. "Detective, you did a great job."
Devon says standing behind the detective.
The female detective then turns around with
a serious look on her face, then smiles.
Handing Devon the case of money, "it's
what I do sir, my job can be dangerous." She
says. Devon stepping closer to her. "That's
what I count on to feel safe." Devon then
kisses the female detective. Smiling after
the kiss, she smiles and walks away. "I got
to go." She says. "Hey…" Devon calls.
Tossing her a stack of cash from the case,
then smacks her on the ass, "Don't spend it
all in one place." She stuffs the cash into
her panties, smiles and walks away. Devon
takes the case of money and puts it in the
trunk of his car, parked in the garage on the
7th floor. "Part one   done, now to close

the show." Devon says to himself heading towards the lobby.

By this time Mr. Whitmen was meeting the escort at the bar located in the casino lobby. Leaning on the bar Mr. Whitmen says to the escort. "You know, I don't remember your name." The escort sipping his drink, "I told you already, but what's in a name? I could just make up one, you wouldn't know the difference." " My name does not matter; I just want to have some fun tonight. No strings, no names, no stress." The escort says finishing off his drink.

Chest not Checkers

Mr. Whitmen stood with an amazed look on his face. "Well, I understand that. So, where do we begin to have fun?" Mr. Whitmen asked. The escort eating the cherry from his drink asks, "Where can we go to be alone. I thought you ran this pace?" Do you have a room or something?" the escort added. Mr. Whitmen touching to escorts shoulder, "sure, let's go. I have a suite with a great view." As the two walked to the elevator, the security camera is following them from the lobby to the suite. Thanks to my connection in the security control room. As the two men enter the suite, Kenny takes over the filming. Kenny is hiding in the   bedroom closet as the two starts kissing and fondling each other and …..Well you get the picture. After Mr.Whitmen, and the escort finish their romp in the suite. Kenny contacts Devon. "Hey Devon, we have the footage we need. Sex drugs, the whole thing." Devon on the other end of the phone smiles, "Cool, meet me in the lobby. We need to set this thing up now." Devon then calls the casino operator to ring the penthouse suite for Mr. Whitmen.   The operator rings the suite and Mr. Whitmen answers while getting dressed. "Hello…" Mr. Whitmen says. "Mr. Whitmen, I need to speak with you, I'm at the front desk."   Mr. Whitmen a little preoccupied says, "Look Devon, I don't have a lot of time, but I'll be there in a minute."   As, the   two meet at the front desk, Mr. Whitmen was all smiles reaching to shake Devon's hand. "Devon what seems to be the matter, I'm really bust tonight." Devon ignoring the hand shake, "let's talk in the ballroom, this is something you would want to hear." As they walk into the ballroom, the footage that was recorded that day was playing on the big screen. Mr. Whitmen looked as if he seen a ghost. He started sweating heavily. Undoing his tie, yelling," What the hell is this, what's going on Devon. What is this shit?" Devon slowly sat down at a table, crossed his legs and lit a cigar. After blowing a smoke ring, "Mr. Whitmen, this is a stick up of sorts. See, I have footage of you doing some pretty questionable things. I mean some things that would cause   you to lose a lot.

Family is very important in a man's world of success and power. I don't know how you kept the fact that you're gay from them. Not to mention that you use and deal drugs to your high rollers. There are a lot of people that could be hurt behind the information I have." Devon added while puffing the cigar. Very nervous, Mr. Whitmen starts to speak. "Devon, look if this gets out a lot of people and families could be torn apart by this, your playing with fire here!" Devon standing up from the table, holding the cigar between his index finger and middle finger of his left hand points at Mr. Whitmen. In a calm monotone voice says, "This is what makes this so…. What's the word….tangible?" Devon walks around the table towards Mr. Whitmen, standing   nearly nose to nose.

"What are you prepared to do to keep this quiet? There are a lot of things to consider. I mean there are the drugs, the undercover homosexuality, and lets not forget Mr. Stacks." Mr. Whitmen steps back with fear, "What about Mr. Stacks?" Devon smiles and puffs on his cigar. "Well, Mr. Stacks just got busted coming from your suite. I'm sure he thinks you set him up, and that's not a good thing. Mr. Stacks has long arms and can reach anyone, anywhere." "Still sweating, "FUCK!" the yell echoed through out the ballroom. "What do you want from me...? I cannot believe this shit!" Devon walks over to his seat again, "It's very simple; you keep your life, how ever foul it may be. It stays in tact; no one will know a thing about what   went down here

178

today. I'll smooth things over with Mr. Stacks by the time he gets out of prison." Mr. Whitmen with tears in his eyes, he yells," WHAT DO YOU WANT DAMMIT!?" Devon sits back and crosses his legs, "$30,000 per month." Mr. Whitmen looked as if he was going to faint, "$30,000 a month!! Are you crazy? Where am I going to get that kind of money, every month?" " Do I look like I give a dam where you or how you get it? You run this casino; you sell drugs in this casino. Make it happen captin. And let's make this clear, you miss a payment or if something happens to me the footage get out. Plus I will make sure Mr. Stacks knows you set him up. So, don't fuck with me!" Devon yelled. Mr. Whitmen composing himself, "Ok, ok you got it. Anything else?" With a devilish grin Devon says, "I want to be a Casino Host with a company car. The car has to be a current year Mercedes. We keep these arrangements, and we are good. You try to screw me in any way, I will screw you harder." Mr. Whitmen wiping the sweat from his face, "Ok you got a deal. Just keep the lines open for me to re-up the stash." Devon putting out the cigar says, "Deal, but I need to have the first payment tonight. One more thing Sky Jones is mine." Mr. Whitmen laughs and shaking his head, I can't afford her anymore, take the bitch." Devon stands up from the table, as Mr. Stacks walks over to shake hands. Devon looked at the outstretched hand of Mr. Whitmen and pushes   it out of the way as he walks away from Mr. Whitmen.

As Devon walks towards the exit of the ballroom, he sees Sky Jones standing in the doorway with her mouth wide open in disbelief and a single tear trickling down her cheek. She was present during the whole conversation. Sky then looked at Devon walking towards her, "You bastard, stay away from me!" Sky said through heart wrenching sobs. Devon wiped the tears from her face. "Go home Sky, I'll call you later on. Get some rest." Devon said trying to console her. Sky looked into Devon's eyes as if he was a stranger. "What the hell am I going to do Devon? He was my meal ticket out of the bullshit life I once had! What the hell do I go from here?" Sky yelled. "Listen, Sky go home. I'll call

you and everything is going to be o.k."
Devon said trying to calm her down. "O.k.,
Devon." Sky said as she walked away.
Devon turns back to look at Mr. Whitmen,
who was still sitting at the table with his
face in his hands crying like a baby. "Don't
forget our deal, bitch." Devon said as he
walked out.

Devon walks across the casino gaming area,
past the craps table where he could hear the
dealer call out the numbers that are being
rolled. There are casino towns across the
country, hell even the world. They all have
those persons that want more than what was
granted. Greed takes over a man or
woman's mind. Greed consumes a person to
the point they lose who they are. The
money, the bright   lights, the drugs that

seem to be endless. Everyday there is a new face, another person looking to come up. Looking for that pot of gold, at the end of the rainbow. But, if you take away the glitz, the glamour. What you find is the cold hard truth…you make your own luck. You have to know when to get in, and when to get out. What chances to take, a calculated risk is a must. It's a world of its own, and this world will chew you up and spit you out if you let it. I have blended into this world; I have become a part of it. I have gotten out of the game of running drugs; I've washed that parasite off of me only to become a different one. It's the game, you either play it or it plays you.

So, what became of   Devon? The next

well dressed casino employee you see, say to him "Hey Devon, you still getting that money?" If he shakes your hand, smiles, and walks away… then you know I am STILL GETTING THAT MONEY!

THE END

ACKNOWLEDGEMENT

First, I want to thank GOD for bringing me this far in this journey called life. You as my readers would possibly pick up through out my books, that life can be a wild ride. All we can do is keep GOD first in our lives, buckle up and hold on tight. I would like to thank my family for sticking by me through out this whole ordeal of writing this first book so, thank you my mom Deborah for believing in me no matter what I wanted to pursue. I love you, my brother Charles and Tanya, my brother Raymond, my brother Jurall and Tequita, my sister Tanya and Chuck. Thank you to my children; Kevin, Taija, Nicholas, and though she is not my biologically – Amber she is loved just as the others. To my loving fiancée Majja, thank you for believing in me and giving me the time and space needed to over all, become a better man, I love you. I also like to thank Author Miasha and

Rich, thank you Miasha for being there for any questions that I had about writing when I lived in Atlanta, GA and from that my drive for writing grew from your encouragement. The other authors that I have been following behind the scenes, giving me that competitive drive to want to do better. To my hometown of Philadelphia for giving endless memories that will keep me writing for many years to come. To the rest of my family and friends, thank you for being who you are, family. Finally, last but not least my grand mother Florence, I wanted to finish this book while you are still with us. I have done that. I love you. I hope you all enjoy, till next time live, love, and laugh. Enjoy life to the fullest each and every day you have been blessed to rise in the morning.